CHRISTMAS HOPE

CAROLINE WARFIELD

MERLIN'S OWL PRESS

For Sarge and soldiers everywhere who struggle with memories,
especially the Chosin Few,
especially at Christmas

Love shall be our token,
Love be yours and love be mine,
Love to God and all men,
Love for plea and gift and sign.

Love came down at Christmas by Christina Rossetti

PART I

ROSES IN PICARDY

CHAPTER 1

November 1916
The Valley of the Somme, France

"Whoever did this is a dead man." Harry pulled his grandmother's Bible from the mud that pooled inches deep in the trench and began to wipe it off with the filthy sleeve of his uniform. Sick of dirt, sick of death, and sick of the everlasting mud, he loosed a flood of curses.

"What do you care, Wheatly? It isn't as if you ever read the damned thing," McNaughton growled without looking up. The sergeant sat on a seat carved into the trench wall cleaning his rifle. McNaughton, ever meticulous about weaponry, tolerated filth in all other ways including his personal hygiene.

"Doesn't matter. Somebody got into my kit," Harry grumbled.

If he said why it mattered, the company would mock him for a week or more. Dumping the book in the mud had been a prank, and there would be more if he admitted why he cared. He might not read the Bible, but when he looked at it, or touched the cover, it put him back on his grandparent's farm in Saskatchewan.

Harry could almost see flowers on the sill and smell the wheat on the wind and the apple pie baking in the kitchen. For that moment at least, he escaped the rot and colorless muck.

Now, even his Bible lay covered in brown dirt.

He wanted to weep. The losses mounted. This one unleashed the grief he had held back by a thread for days, a toll of the dead too heavy to bear: Simpson, Morin, Reilly, Campeau, Erikson—so many dead in the months of fighting, and they were only thirteen kilometers closer to Germany, thirteen farther from the Somme.

"Damn it, Wheatly, you're depressing me. You look like your dog died. Take the blasted book down to the river and clean it if it matters that much. The Huns aren't shooting at us for now. Ask the lieutenant for a pass," McNaughton told him.

Harry grabbed at the chance. *Anything to get out of the trenches for an afternoon.* He rinsed his hands in the basin of brownish water, wrapped the muddy Bible in a handkerchief that was almost clean, and rummaged through his canvas haversack. Whoever tossed his grandmother's Bible in the mud hadn't taken anything else. The oilcloth sack he kept it in had been opened but was still there.

He tucked the book in his field jacket, grabbed the haversack, and set off. It wasn't hard to find Lieutenant Harvey. Most days he hid in his quarters, a space hollowed out in the trench the size of a large closet. The damned fool had been too green to turn down the commission when offered. A merchant's son from Ottawa, he strutted around like a peacock for a few weeks until he figured out what the rest of them knew. Once they went over the top, a lieutenant's life wasn't worth spit.

Harvey started shaking in his boots once the Battle of the Somme got underway, and he hadn't stopped. He hid in his lair and made life miserable for the rest of them.

"Wheatly. Good. Just what I need." Harvey sat on a campstool in front of a crate doing duty as a desk. "The captain wants someone to carry his report to the British high command in

Querrieu. Wants someone who speaks French." He looked at his desk and mumbled, "As if the brass hats don't already know Hell when they see it."

Harry opened his mouth to object but remembered Querrieu was down river. Still, he hated being Harvey's errand boy. He found no words to explain why he needed to get to the river, at least none the army would understand. He put one arm across his chest and held onto the book.

"Well? Don't just stand there."

"Where's the company clerk? Why don't you send him?" Harry demanded. He didn't try to swallow the insolence. In his mind, Harvey didn't deserve any respect.

"Dysentery. Just follow orders."

"Yes, Sir." He snapped off a cocky salute.

It took Harry two hours to find Captain Mitchell, who had to locate the portfolio, and another twenty minutes to convince the man he needed a pass.

Querrieu is practically to Amiens. "Best make it for a few days," he insisted. *Send me that far, and I'm damned well not coming back the same day.* He managed to invent a reason just needy enough without sounding pathetic and without revealing his true errand: the company needed socks. No direct plea to the quartermaster would actually result in socks, but it sounded good. Harry also reminded the captain twice that he had led a doomed squad into the maw of a Maxim machine gun nest on the man's orders to save the entire company's bacon. Tamping down visions of dying comrades and his rage while he said it took every ounce of his waning supply of self-control.

"Besides, Captain, the shooting isn't likely to begin again in earnest until after the first of the year, spring if we're lucky."

That turned the trick.

He left with a three-day pass, happy to emerge from the everlasting ditches, if nothing else. Another frustrating hour later, he finally accepted that the promised ambulance meant to carry him all the way to Amiens wouldn't be in any shape to move that day. The sun hung low by the time he convinced a mechanic to give him a lift on a motorcycle.

"I can get you to Corbie, but that's it. I'm salvaging some parts and coming straight back. You'll have to get a farmer to take you the rest of the way."

"Or a boatman."

What was left of Corbie lay where the Ancre met the Somme. He hugged the old Bible close. It would do.

NUDGING HER BOAT, a smallish version of the high-backed *barque à cornet* of Picardy, toward the quay at St-Leu, Rosemarie Legrand struggled against the current. She blinked up at the towers of Amiens' massive cathedral looming on its rise behind the ancient houses of St-Leu, the medieval quarter, and breathed a prayer.

Does God answer desperate widows? Or has he turned his back on me like everyone else?

Whether the prayer or a deft movement of her pole made the difference, the *barque* moved sharply forward and came alongside in a smooth movement. She leapt out and tied the boat before reaching down to lift out her son.

Marcel smiled back, looking up with eyes too big for his two-year-old face. She grabbed his hand and carried her bundle toward the other vendors. Cold stares kept her to the fringes. Hatred made her stomach churn. She wouldn't be here at all, but she had to have Marcel's tonic. The rattle in his chest had returned as soon as summer faded, and she feared it might worsen in the coming winter. Food shortages would bring buyers, even ones who wouldn't otherwise speak to her. Her pathetic little pile of late harvest root vegetables and dried fish would bring a few coins. She tried not to think about how the two of them would manage in coming months.

"You come here, brazen as can be? Where do you get the nerve?" The one person Rosemarie most hoped to avoid stormed toward her. Her sister-in-law, Sabine, eyes blazing, pointed an accusatory finger. "You won't be so smug when we take my brother's son from you."

Rosemarie hugged Marcel more firmly and glared back. "The authorities sided with me!"

"We'll see what they say when you starve this winter and let the boy suffer. We'll see!" Sabine pointed at the boy and waved her arm off in disgust. She stalked off, muttering, "Don't buy that Hun-lover's wares. She probably poisons them!"

A few hours later bells from churches across Amiens rang the noon Angelus when Rosemarie trudged back across the cathedral square toward St-Leu and her little boat with her drowsy son on one hip. The sight of the great shrine cowering behind monstrous walls of sandbags, its exquisite carvings in hiding and its windows blocked from both sun and shellfire, roiled her belly. She felt as if the ancient building contained within itself all the suffering and the growing pile of losses at the hands of the hated Germans. No matter what her sister-in-law told people, she was no German sympathizer.

Rosemarie sped up, anxious for the safety of home now that she had a precious vial of tonic for Marcel wrapped in linen inside her pouch. The apothecary had not met her eyes and spoke no more words than necessary, but he took her coin readily enough. Monsieur Pelletier might believe Sabine's lies, but he would never begrudge Marcel his medicine. She had what she needed, and she didn't have to face the good people of Amiens for a few more months.

Marcel lay on a pile of blankets while his mother put out into the Somme, punting toward *les hortillonnages*, the floating gardens of Amiens, a maze of islands and canals—and her little plot, her haven of safety. She crossed the Somme and guided her *barque* unerringly to the rivulet that would lead her home. The sight of an oncoming boat in the distance gave her movements some urgency, her taste for human interaction being used up that day.

As she swung her *barque* toward the channel, movement in the water caught her eye. A brown object swirled in an eddy along the bank of the Somme and lodged in a tangle of roots and twigs where the channel opened into the river. Closer inspection made her drag the pole to slow the boat. On impulse, she reached down and scooped up a filthy book, its sodden pages dripping down her front.

One more sad ruin. Pity to waste such a thing.

She laid it on the bottom of the boat and pushed on forward, impatient to get home, weaving her way between islands and boat docks. Twenty feet from her goal, she let her pole drag. A green two-man *barque à cornet* bobbed next to the steps to her plot. Its green color and the cross affixed to its raised stern identified its owner. She swallowed the urge to turn around—an insane idea since the narrowness of the channel made it almost impossible—and took her time tying up.

When she gathered the sleeping Marcel and shouldered her packet, she tossed a rag over the sodden book. Procrastination while she climbed the steps toward her house on leaden feet wouldn't protect her from what waited there.

Abbé Desjardin watched her from his seat upon one of the wooden chairs in front of her house, his pristine white collar in stark contrast to his black cassock, his expression morose. He shook his grizzled head. "If I had known you finally stirred yourself to come into town, Rosemarie, I could have saved myself a trip. I'm glad to know you do leave this place. What I don't know is why you don't come to Mass on Sunday."

She sank into the seat next to him and prepared for a familiar argument.

CHAPTER 2

"Hey! Wait!" Harry shouted himself hoarse.

He saw the woman pull his grandmother's book from the river, but she went on and didn't stop. It took several moments and more coin to convince the boatman to follow her down the narrow channel.

She disappeared into one of the innumerable side channels before they turned. He sank back with a groan, but the boatman never hesitated. Sharp right, a lazy left, and another sharp turn and the boat eased up next to two small boats, one with peeling paint and a second one painted a garish green and sporting—of all things—a crucifix on the raised stern.

"Why are you stopping?" Harry demanded, straining for the answer. He had never been so grateful that his mother insisted her children be bilingual as he had that day. His French hadn't failed him yet, but the boatman's mumbling challenged it.

"You follow Madame Legrand, do you not?" The man spat over the side.

"You knew who it was?"

A curt nod was the response. "I wish you well of her."

"I don't want your Madame Legrand. I want my book," Harry

said, climbing out. He leapt up the four steps and came to an abrupt halt.

After months in a brown haze—a universe of men in khaki trapped in mud walls—a riot of color drove the breath from his body and coherent thought from his mind. A tiny cottage painted bright blue with yellow shutters and red window boxes dominated the scene. A small patch of grass, still green in late fall, spread in front of it, cut in two by blue-grey stepping-stones. Trees nestled around the cottage still held on to leaves that had muted into dark oranges and reds, the last remnant of autumn color. They were, he realized, the first trees he'd seen in weeks that hadn't been reduced to ragged stumps by shellfire or stripped for fuel. A longing to see the place in spring when the window boxes and the pots below them would be lush with flowers overtook him. He stared, mouth agape.

"Monsieur?" A lilting voice penetrated his distraction.

He shook his head to clear it only to face another wonder. A woman peered at him through hazel eyes lit with intelligence and wide with curiosity. Brown hair escaped her efforts to tie it back and curled waywardly around her face. She wasn't, he supposed, pretty in the way of the delicate flowers of Ottawa society that had attracted him in the past, but at that moment, he found her quite the most enchanting creature he had ever seen.

"Monsieur, may I help you?" the vision repeated.

Get a grip, Harry. He wondered—no, he knew—he had been too long without a woman's company.

"Pardon me," he sputtered at last. "Are you Madame Legrand?"

Madame. Married. Remember that Harry and stop salivating like some animal.

"I am. Who wishes to know?"

Harry saw a man rise from his seat behind the woman and come to stand at her shoulder. *Her husband? No, he's dressed like—* Harry gaped. *A priest?*

"You— I— That is, I think you have my book," he stuttered. Heat crept up his neck, and all self-confidence fled.

"I beg your pardon?"

Both of them gaped at him as if he were the village idiot.

Manners, his grandmother always advised, worked best in "any uncomfortable encounter."

He yanked off his service cap and began again. "I'm sorry. It has been a trying day. I am Corporal Henry Wheatly, and—" *Oh hell! Just spit it out, Harry.* "I lost my Bible."

The priest raised his eyebrows at that. "You ought to have more care than to carry sacred texts into a war zone, soldier."

"Try telling my grandmother that, Father..."

"I am *Abbé* Desjardin. Your grandmother is Protestant, no?" The old man looked amused.

Even Madame Legrand's eyes lit with humor. Her lips... Harry thought he best ignore her lips, laughing or otherwise.

"Methodist," Harry replied.

Of course, she is. Only a Methodist would think a Bible belonged in the trenches. Catholics keep them locked up, his father always said.

"And how did you lose this Bible?" the woman asked.

"I dropped it while I was washing it."

"You wash your Bible?" the priest asked, looking rather like an astonished owl, all bushy white brows, and sharp black eyes.

"Not usually." He ran a shaking hand through his hair and across the back of his neck. "Let me begin at the beginning."

As he did, his eyes kept straying to the woman who listened earnestly to his story. The warmth of her eyes encouraged him to tell them more about his attachment to the thing than he intended. He told them the whole sad tale of the prank, the book, his orders, and the frustrating trip thus far.

"So when he wouldn't wait, I had to wash the book along the way," he concluded, still fixed on the woman's eyes. "I started by dipping a rag in the river, but it made a rather large mess, and I hung it over the side. When the current jerked the boat sideways, the book flew out of my hand. It kept floating in the current farther and farther out of reach, until I saw you pull it from the water."

"Ah. The big brown book. Yes," the woman began.

A cry interrupted her. When she turned, Harry noticed a small boy sitting in front of the cottage rubbing his eyes.

Madame Legrand lifted the boy to her hip and came back. "I'm afraid it is quite ruined. I hoped to dry it and see what could be done."

"Excellent idea, my dear Rosemarie," the priest said. "Even a Protestant text should be treated with respect, if read with care." He spun toward Harry. "No offence intended, corporal. You aren't British."

"Canadian."

"Ah, Courcellette and Thiepval. We have been given to understand your troops are wild men."

Harry's mouth clamped shut. Neither word conjured thoughts he wished to share with this gnome of a clergyman. "My Bible, Madame Legrand?" he ground out through clenched teeth.

The shock of a baby thrust into his arms and the feel of a woman brushing past left him unable to speak further. He watched her swift descent to the tethered boat and graceful ascent up the steps in silence. She held out a sodden mess in both hands, his precious book wilted and as muddy as ever.

"As you can see, Monsieur, it has sustained damage. Is it possible you could return in a few days? I could dry it for you and attempt to salvage it."

Harry had to think. If he put it in the oilcloth for the return trip, it would only mold. In the trench—or even at camp when they rotated out—he had no hope of drying it.

Just when he reached the silent conclusion that he may as well leave it since it was lost to him in any case, the body of the little boy curled against his shoulder sent sweet warmth through him. The smell of baby and growing plants, the scent of life and growth, filled his senses. If he left the book, he had an excuse to return to this oasis of hope.

He raised his eyes to the woman's, meeting the concern he saw there. "I can do that," he said, although he had no idea when or how. "I may be able stop on my way back," he mused, although he doubted his three-day pass gave her enough time to repair the damage.

"Your treasure will be safe with me while you fulfill your duties," she replied.

His duties.

"Yes, I have reports to deliver. I had best continue." He turned to the channel and realized for the first time that the boatman had abandoned him. *Damn! He must have left as soon as I scrambled out of his boat.*

He spun back. "I fear I am stranded, Madame Legrand."

Abbé Desjardin snorted. "Benoit Clotier is a selfish bastard. He took your coin and saw to his own comfort. You destination is Amiens? Mine is as well. I will take you there."

"Querrieu, British headquarters," Harry replied, visions of discipline for dereliction of duty making his heart sink.

The priest shrugged. "Ten miles only. I will take you there."

Harry handed the boy back to his mother with great reluctance. An irrational urge to hold onto the little one, as if some spark of life would be torn away when he let go, swept over him. He quickly stifled it, but the feeling confused him. Even leaving his grandmother's Bible caused less of a wrench. The *abbé* waited at his boat impatiently, and Harry had no excuse to linger.

I will come back, he told himself. *I will come back.*

Moments later, Harry leaned elbows on his knees from his seat at the front of the boat and let the swish of the priest's punting soothe his nerves. The maze of rivulets linked dozens of tiny islands, lush with plant life and dotted with a rainbow of small houses. Stumps gave evidence to the desperate need for fuel. They passed vegetable plots, empty now but obviously harvested with care. An apple tree almost made him weep.

"She is a good woman." The priest's voice startled him out of his languid mood.

"I have no reason to doubt that," Harry said over his shoulder. "She was very kind."

"Others see it differently."

Harry had no reply to that. The woman's reputation was none of his business.

"She makes no effort to help herself."

Harry turned then and looked directly into knowing black eyes. "What are you saying?"

"She hides in *les hortillonnages*—this maze of islands—while her sister-in-law, Sabine, spreads venom." The old man shook his head. "I tell her she should come to Mass on Sundays and hold her head high, but she refuses. At very least, the ladies of Amiens must see her caring for the little one. He is sickly, and Sabine accuses Rosemarie of neglect. That snake will try to take him because she can't have one of her own."

"What does Madame Legrand's husband say about that?"

"Dead these six months. No great loss, God forgive me for saying. It was a dark day for little Rosemarie Jacques when she married into that family."

Harry turned forward, digesting the *abbé's* words. *A widow.* A surge of pleasure made him feel foolish. The desire accompanying it shamed him. It sounded as if the woman had enough problems.

Silence stretched between them while the priest guided his boat toward the Somme and turned into the stream.

"There is something you should know if you come to Amiens. Benoit Clotier will put it about that you visited Rosemarie Legrand. Word may even reach Querrieu."

Harry turned back to look at the priest. "And?"

Abbé Desjardin sighed deeply. "Raoul Legrand's last gift to his wife. He screamed to his family that Rosemarie was a German sympathizer."

"Why on earth?"

"A deserter, no more than a boy, washed up in *les hortillonnages,* half drowned and wounded. Rosemarie pulled him in and tended his wounds, good Christian woman that she is. Because of foul weather, it was two days before she could get him to authorities in Amiens. Neighbors, who would have let the boy die if they could have, reported her and sent word to Raoul. By the time he came home two weeks later, he had convinced himself she had taken a German lover who fled to her when he was shot. He raged at her and savaged her reputation before returning to the front. He died a week later."

"And people believed him."

"In wartime, truth is often the first casualty," the old man said sadly. "That's why she has to help herself." He brightened as if struck by an idea. "It might help if she was seen with one of our heroic allies."

Harry's head shot up. "What are you implying?"

The gnome of a man shrugged as he crossed to the river's edge near headquarters. Boys rushed to help the *abbé* tie up his boat.

Standing on the embankment, he looked steadily at Harry. "You can imagine the people are desperate for a respite, and so the community will hold its traditional Christmas market in two weeks." The black eyes scrutinized Harry's blue ones. He seemed to like what he saw. "If Rosemarie were to attend in the company of one of our brave allied soldiers, it might put her in a better light."

Harry choked. "Or make it worse!"

"Perhaps, but she's a widow now, and there is no reason why she cannot enjoy the company of a soldier—one on our side. Doing her patriotic duty."

Loping toward the castle that had been commandeered for

the high command, Harry decided the old priest was crazy. Perhaps Harry was too. He couldn't get the picture of Rosemarie Legrand walking at his side on his arm out of his imagination. It would not happen. He would be back in the trenches in two days.

Before I go, I'll see her one more time. That I can do.

CHAPTER 3

Two days of sun, a gift in November, helped, but the stranger's book still lay damp and wilted on the rock where Rosemarie arranged it every morning. Evenings, she laid it on the floor in front of her stove during the hours she burned her precious supply of fuel.

Will he come back after it? She knew the fragility of hope. He would return to his unit and may not be able to return. Even now, with a lull in the action holding, men died. Soon enough, the carnage would begin again. Somehow, it became vital to her to rescue his book as if it too had become a victim of war.

The third morning, rain poured down, and she kept Marcel—and the Bible—inside. Rain pelted her few windows, masking all sight and sound. When a knock on her door rang out, she jumped. A second more insistent hammering started as she reached for it. She yanked it open to find the Canadian corporal looming over her, water dripping from his service cap onto his soaked uniform coat. She grabbed his hand and pulled him inside.

Let the nasty neighbors think what they want. I won't let him catch his death on my doorstep.

"I am on my way back to my unit," he said, blue eyes bleak. "I thought I would check on my book. The boatman—" he began, turning to point. "Damn it!"

Through the still open door, Rosemarie saw that the wretched man had already pushed off and abandoned his passenger. The corporal must have paid in advance. She shook her head. *Will this one ever learn?*

The corporal looked at her sheepishly. "Apologies, Madame, but how am I going to get back?" he asked.

Rosemarie had a moment of panic and quickly squelched it. *At least with the boatman gone I don't have to find room for another large, wet male in my kitchen.*

"You seem to be stuck here. Take off that hat and your coat, corporal, while I start a fire." She handed him a towel.

When he ran his long and gracefully formed fingers through his wet hair, he looked boyish and befuddled. Sympathy took over.

"Boots, Corporal Wheatly," she added, pointing to the door. She didn't need mud tracked across her kitchen.

"Harry," he said, applying the towel to thick auburn hair. "My name is Harry."

When he obliged, she saw to the fire.

She opened the damper and tossed a few sticks of wood into the belly of her tiny stove. The inconvenient man cost her fuel she could ill afford. She dreaded cutting another tree and facing the choice between fruit and fuel.

Worse, she grumbled to herself, *the neighbors will gossip until it reaches Sabine soon enough.* He also brought one other worry. *How will I get him to his unit?*

That will have to keep until the rain stops. She stood, brushed bark off her hands, and sighed. She'd invited him in. She may as well enjoy conversation with an adult.

The man stood with his back to her, peering down at his Bible where it lay on the windowsill. "Still damp," he said.

"It needs more sunny days," she replied. "Now that I've lit a fire, I'll move it closer, but first, sit. My kitchen is too small."

He did as she asked, bending his large frame to her little table.

She walked around to fill a kettle. "Tea will warm you."

While water boiled, she fetched the book and laid it open on a small stool closer to the stove, opening it to a section she had not yet dried. She bustled over to bring her two best cups from the cupboard and placed them in front of him. The man's tight smile made her wonder if he felt as awkward as she did. She spooned some of her meager supply of tea into a teapot.

"Where is your son?" he asked.

"Napping."

Uncomfortable moments passed while she peered into the kettle which, being watched, refused to boil.

"Your French is excellent, Harry," she said to fill the silence.

A smile lit his face and warmed her heart. "My mother insisted we all speak fluently. 'You have to speak to all the neighbors,' she would say."

"Does everyone in Canada speak two languages?" she asked. She considered asking him to make use of her personal name and decided against it. The kitchen made them intimate enough.

He shook his head. "No. Some think we must enforce a single language. The Province of Ontario forbad teaching in French a few years ago. Bishop Fallon, good Irishman that he is, agreed and forbad it even in Catholic schools. The outcry has been loud, and continues. My mother calls them 'bloody idiots,'" he told her.

"Clergy can be narrow minded," she said. *More than this man can possibly know.* With the exception of *Abbé* Desjardin, the clergy of Amiens had been quick to judge her, quick to believe Raoul's accusations. *Hypocritical fools!*

"Your priest seemed more humane," he said as if he read her mind.

"He has known me since I was a child. He is wise and kind. Not all of them are."

"He said..." the corporal broke off, coloring brightly.

Rosemarie stood abruptly and busied herself making tea. She didn't think she wanted to know what the *abbé* told this man, but she may as well get it out. At least he wasn't talking to Sabine.

"What exactly did *Abbé* Desjardin tell you?" she asked over her shoulder, the words sour in her mouth.

"That you've been unfairly judged. That you chose charity over self-regard and have paid for it dearly."

Her shoulders relaxed, the sensation of comfort rolling up her neck and down her back. "He's a good man," she murmured.

"How did you find the German?" he asked.

His interest sounded genuine, but she breathed deeply before answering. "I was fishing in the Somme. Early mornings are best, and I was alone with Marcel. When I started for home, I found him caught in the weeds, just where I found your Bible. Things catch there often. This time, it was a human being. I pulled him out."

"Why didn't you take him into Amiens?"

"I struggled to manage a wounded man and Marcel both, and I needed to dock quickly. Home was closer. I would have stopped at another cabin, but none looked occupied, and most of them would have let the boy die." She sank back into her chair. "He died anyway. My so-called generosity was for nothing and brought me the undying contempt of my neighbors."

"So the *abbé* said. He also said you are hurting yourself by hiding away."

"He wants me at Sunday Mass. Typical priest."

"He thinks the ladies of Amiens need to witness what a good mother you are. For your protection."

She snorted, an unladylike sound she didn't regret. "Those hags believe Sabine. Why should I have to put on a show for them?"

The corporal watched her intently, his blue eyes lit with curiosity, until she began to squirm in her seat. She wondered if he found her attractive. Raoul's eyes had taken on a predatory gleam whenever desire drove him. This man's eyes had a different sort of warmth.

"The *abbé* also thinks you would do well to visit the Christmas market with Marcel."

She shook her head to deny it. "I won't put Marcel in that position."

"He thinks it would be better if you were on the arm of—his words—a 'brave allied soldier.'" He grinned ruefully.

Rosemarie choked on her tea so badly the corporal jumped to his feet to pat her back until she regained control.

"The old reprobate!" she growled when she could.

"BETTER?" Harry watched the woman with concern, profoundly sorry he told her the priest's idea. Obviously, it horrified her. *Of course it did. Why would she want to parade around Amiens with a perfect stranger?*

He rubbed circles on her back, unable to pull his hand away, until she hitched one shoulder and pushed him away.

"Sorry. I didn't want you to choke." He sat back down and studied his hands for a few moments.

"What did you say to *Abbé* Desjardin's ludicrous idea?"

"I told him I didn't see how it would help your reputation. He —" Harry looked directly at her then, choosing his words carefully. "He said a widow might respectably walk out with a man, and that giving attention to 'one on our side'—again, his words— might show your patriotic duty."

Their eyes held for several moments. In the silence, Harry came to an uncomfortable admission. He had hoped she would like the idea. He doubted he could get away during the Christmas market, but he had hoped she might want him to.

She blinked at last and looked across the room. "*Abbé* Desjardin is a doddering old fool."

A toddler's cries saved him from answering. Madame Legrand scurried upstairs faster than she needed to. *Eager to get away from me, no doubt.* He listened to her footsteps above. Given the size of the cottage, the upper floor must be a tiny loft.

In the silent kitchen, Harry tried to focus on his surroundings rather than his disordered thoughts. Unfortunately, what he saw brought him little comfort. The place looked clean but spartan to the point of poverty. The box from which she had taken wood for the stove held two small pieces. A few jars of preserved vegetables sat on open shelves above the sink. He knew of the food shortages—everyone did—but there ought to be more here for a woman and her son. Perhaps he just couldn't see it. Perhaps she could ill afford her kindness. Guilt crept in.

He poured another cup of tea. The leaves had been fresh and the brew strong. Even the teapot reproached him. He feared she had used her last. The temptation to peer into her tea caddy to check if there was more overtook him.

Padding to the counter in stocking feet, Harry stole a glance in the caddy. She hadn't used the last but very close to it. *Can she get more?* He had no idea how bad things were in the city or whether there was tea to be had.

He cocked an ear to the murmur of voices, a mother soothing a little one. Hearing that his hostess remained occupied, he opened a box on the counter to find half a loaf of bread and then a cupboard door where there were two jars of flour and little else. *How are they surviving? Fish?*

The sound of her feet on the steps made him jerk around to lean his backside against the counter. He crossed one ankle over the other, trying to look nonchalant.

"All is well with the little one?" he asked, as innocently as he could manage. He gestured toward the toddler she carried.

She eyed him dubiously but made no criticism. "He woke early. He will be irritable after dinner," she replied. The smile she gave the boy took any sting out of her words. She glanced past him to the window. "The rain has stopped."

So it had. Harry's heart sank. He didn't want to leave, but duty demanded it. He had to impose again. He had to go back. "I'm afraid I have to trouble you."

"How far is your unit? Are you above Albert?"

"Nearly."

She worried her lower lip between even teeth. "I can't get that far up river and back before dark. Will you be in trouble if you don't go directly?"

His heart leapt. *Is she inviting me to stay?* He calmed the storm upending his mind. He had to go back, however tempting the urge to stay. As if that weren't enough, he couldn't impose on the household's slender resources any further.

"Yes. My pass ends today."

"If I take you back to Amiens, can you find your way from there?"

He shrugged. There would likely be trucks going back and forth. *I ought to have hitched a ride this morning.* Hiring a boatman had been an extravagance; one he knew had its roots in a desire to see this place again. *This place and this woman.*

Still, they didn't hurry away. She put a crock on the stove and fed the boy, fish stew as Harry had guessed. She didn't offer him any and looked embarrassed by that. Harry busied himself pulling on boots and coat, trying not to notice.

"Will you take your Bible?" she asked after she had bundled the little boy into his jacket.

Will I? Nothing has changed, not really. He still couldn't dry it where he was going. He caught her eyes, and for a moment, they held him transfixed. *Hazel,* he thought, *and full of life.*

"No," he said at last. "I'll come back for it."

The woman nodded and made no reply. They traveled to the ancient city without further speech. She held the boat steady while he got out, and then pushed away. He raised a hand to wave. Her only reply was a little nod. He stood for a long time watching them go.

I'll come back...

CHAPTER 4

"Thank goodness Wheatly's back. Now, he can read us bedtime stories again."

Harry sank deeper into the shadows, leaned against the clay wall, and kept his eyes on the weapon he was cleaning on McNaughton's orders. He scowled at Walker's snide comment, but the bastard earned enough laughter from their fellows to urge him to continue anyway. The troops were all squirrelly because their rotation in the trenches had been extended two more weeks.

"Where's your book, Wheatly? Did it float down the ooze to the Frenchie trench? Did you look there? I hear they have wine over in their trenches. Is that why you were gone so long?"

"Yeah, Harry, how about the wine?" Martens teased.

Harry saw Martens as a brave soldier who knew his duty and did it, unlike Walker, a shirker and coward of the first order. *Rosemarie Legrand exercises more courage just getting through one day than Jonas Walker showed me in the eighteen months I've known him.*

He shook his head to clear the thought and smiled at Martens' muddy grin.

"Best ever," he said, inviting a glare from Walker. "Tasted like my grandfather's best. I should thank whoever dropped that book in the ooze. Gave me a chance to visit the neighbors."

Any doubt he had that Walker had been the one to ruin his grandmother's Bible evaporated under the man's sour expression.

Michaels, skinny and nervous, their youngest and in Harry's opinion most naïve member, went wide-eyed. "What's it like in the Frenchie trench, Harry?"

"Same as here, Michaels, clay, dirt, and putty. Even the wine looked brown. I think they make it from prunes. Tasted fine though." The laughter turned friendly, and Harry went on. "One of them tried to convince me the walls of their trench were chocolate, but I didn't fall for it."

The laughter became uproarious, the men too desperate for humor to resist. Walker stalked off to harass someone else. Harry kept working.

The comments continued, each one more ribald and lascivious than the next. Harry wondered what they would think if they knew about Rosemarie Legrand. He didn't like to consider what might be said.

"Enough, you dirt bags," McNaughton growled at last. "Harvey sent him on a pointless errand. That's where he was. Now, get back to work before I assign you to latrine duty for a month."

Harry glanced up to see McNaughton watching him under lowered lashes.

"How was Amiens really?" the sergeant asked. "Meet any Mamzells? I hear the ones in that little house on Rue St. Roch are ooh la la."

"Why, sergeant, you know the brass hats frown on that kind of fraternization. I would never." Harry winked, a slow lascivious gesture he hoped would satisfy McNaughton's salacious curiosity.

"If I had your know-how, Wheatly," the sergeant said, "I'd be cozying up to the captain. Can never tell when he'll be wanting a college boy who reads and knows French."

McNaughton no sooner got those words out than a shaft of sunlight cut into the trench, bathing Harry's side in light. He turned his face up, letting it warm his face, and sucked in a breath. Just as quickly, the clouds closed in, and the gloom descended.

"Shite," McNaughton spat. "God—if there is one—has a nasty sense of humor."

Harry couldn't argue with that. The little house on its floating island had been like that, a shaft of light to warm him and then cut off as soon as he touched it.

A week later, the sun still hid, visions of Rosemarie Legrand still haunted his nights, and the numbing boredom of army life still threatened to crush his soul. When he first reached France, he had found solace in writing poetry, but he had long run out of metaphors for death, synonyms for brown, and images of darkness. Martens made jokes, Walker abused his fellows, and a particularly damaged private captured and tortured rats. They all coped as best as they could. Harry was sure he had begun to go mad the morning it occurred to him that even the fighting would be preferable to the long slow annihilation of those trapped in the hell of the trenches.

He began to withdraw into the pictures in his mind, leaning his head against the trench wall and closing his eyes when he could. The images rose as soon as he did: the robin's egg blue of the cottage the first time he saw it, Marcel smiling up at him, sun streaming into Rosemarie's kitchen and lighting the highlights in her hair. That last one could not be real, as it had poured rain when he was there. He didn't care. He no longer knew if the woman had been real or a figment of his imagination. He only knew the vision of her kept his soul alive.

"Wheatly!"

He blinked to clear his vision. It didn't help. The dark haze made it hard to distinguish faces. He knew the voice though.

"Quit yer daydreaming about them wimmen in Amiens," McNaughton barked. "Captain wants you."

Harry pushed to his feet. "You sure about that?"

"Just go see the man, you lucky sod, or I'll do it for you."

ROSEMARIE KNEW it for the fool's errand it was as soon as she walked into the Christmas Market in the cathedral square holding her son's little hand. A woman pulled her little girl away as if to protect her from contamination. She told *Abbé* Desjardin how wrong he was, but she went anyway, lured by the old priest's promise of protection and of sweets for Marcel—something she could never give him. His note that morning, brought by an openly insulting Benoit Clotier, had been particularly insistent that she come in the evening, "...so that Marcel can see the candle lighting." *Would this be easier on the arm of an allied soldier?* Rosemarie refused to hope for that.

She searched the crowd for the priest. A man in khaki caught her attention, and her heart gave a leap. She chided that unruly organ for its foolishness. The Canadian had gone back to his unit, and she had no word from him. His book, as clean and dry as she could make it, lay on her windowsill in the unlikely event he might come to claim it. Expecting him to appear in front of the cathedral made her feel ridiculous.

The market had little of its pre-war appeal. The sandbags encasing parts of the medieval church that towered over the square reminded them all that fighting could break out at any moment. No hams hung from the butcher's booth. Cakes and sweets were smaller and fewer and less gaily decorated. She had no money to purchase them, but the *abbé* had promised. It would wait.

A group of laughing and pointing children clustered around a puppet theatre on the far side of the square. Though yards away, she could see Guignol, everyone's favorite puppet character, in heated action with a gendarme.

Marcel could hear them too, and he tugged her hand. She allowed him to lead her to the puppets and lifted him so he could see from the back of the crowd of children. One or two alert mothers pulled their precious darlings away with a glare, but for the most part, families were too absorbed in the show to pay attention to a despised widow and her unfortunate son.

Marcel laughed along with everyone else, and the sound soothed her heart. It had been weeks since she had heard it.

All too soon, the puppets finished their antics, and the crowd of children dispersed. Alone in the midst of a bustling crowd with no money to spend, Rosemarie felt an urge to leave, to retreat to the safety of her little house.

Don't be a coward! Besides, you told the abbé *you would meet him.*

Music wafted over the crowd from the massive front doors of the cathedral. The promised candle lighting would be by the ancient crèche, as would the carolers and perhaps the *abbé*. She led Marcel toward the church.

The distinctive figure of the priest emerged from the gloom, his head lifted upward, deep in conversation with someone. A strangled gasp almost choked her when they stepped into the circle of light, and the Canadian came into focus leaning over the *abbé*. Highlights flickered off the auburn hair across his forehead. He wore a crisp clean uniform this time, and his boots shone. When his eyes found her, she thought they brightened, but she quickly dismissed that as a trick of the candlelight.

"Ah, Rosemarie!" *Abbé* Desjardin said. "Look who surprised me this evening—our Corporal Wheatly."

He made a great show of introducing them for the benefit of the gossips of Amiens, going on at length about "when we met" and "do you remember?" Rosemarie knew it for nonsense and didn't listen in any case. She had eyes and ears for the corporal alone. The heat in his blue eyes told her he felt the same.

"Good evening, Madame Legrand. It is a privilege to meet you again," he said, a slow smile spreading across his face.

Singing resumed, and the four of them listened for a while until the *abbé* took Marcel's hand to lead him toward the ancient crèche. When the corporal offered his arm, she took it.

"Did you have a crèche in your home, corporal?" she asked, leaning closer to be heard over the singing.

"Harry," he corrected.

She couldn't resist a smile.

"We did," he replied. "My mother found it an endearing custom and insisted on it. Does that surprise you, Madame Legrand?"

"Rosemarie," she murmured.

He leaned closer to hear. "What did you say?"

"My name is Rosemarie."

"I'm honored," he whispered back, tugging her a bit closer to his side.

Cold night air stung her cheeks, but warmth flowed through her middle at the rumble of his voice close to her ear and the sudden trace of musk and male when she breathed in. She shivered, unable to look at him, putting a few inches between them, by turning to grip her son's hand and join the *abbé* in explaining the figures and their story.

"Who that?" Marcel asked, pointing to the statue of the youngest shepherd in the back, the one carrying a lamb on his shoulder.

"That is my favorite," Harry said, his voice reverberating over her shoulder, echoing in her chest.

Marcel, Rosemarie, and *Abbé* Desjardin all turned to him.

"He is also a shepherd," Harry went on, "but he's late because he stopped to help the little lamb who fell into the brambles. My mother always said that was me. Late for every event."

"I like," Marcel said, looking back at the statue.

They all stared at the crèche, letting the music and the candles cast a mantle of tranquility over them. A strident voice shattered Rosemarie's peace moments later.

"You dare show your face at this church?" Sabine shrilled during a lull in the singing. She spoke loud enough to make sure as many people as possible heard.

Before Rosemarie could respond, *Abbé* Desjardin spoke for her. "Madame Legrand has as much a right to the church's grace as any woman here. She has kindly offered to give my friend, Corporal Wheatly, a tour of our treasure. Who are you to say otherwise?"

Sabine glared at the priest, and Rosemarie thought she might insult him, but the shrew backed down. Her eyes dropped to Marcel, a ravenous sort of expression as she examined the little boy closely.

"Marcel looks thin," she said for want of anything worse to say.

"He eats as well as any child in Picardy does these days," Rosemarie responded. "No more." *Let Sabine make what she wants of that. A "German lover's child" would grow fat, would he not?*

Sabine shot her a hateful look. "Corporal Wheatly you say?" she asked, turning to Harry. "I hope someone tells you the truth about this woman."

"I believe someone has," he replied, looking at the priest.

"Then I wish you well," she spat and flounced off.

"That woman will choke on her own bile, one day," the *abbé* said, shaking his head.

Rosemarie thought he spoke a bit louder than normal as well, as if they all performed for an audience. The faces Rosemarie saw staring seemed to hold curiosity if not sympathy and less hostility than before.

"Thank you for giving my friend a tour of the cathedral, Rosemarie, tonight of all nights. I would accompany you, but I have pressing business." The priest turned to leave. "Oh, and, corporal, don't forget to make sure Marcel gets his promised sweet cake."

The priest left before Rosemarie could stop him, leaving her with the stranger who had washed up on her island and upended her life.

CHAPTER 5

She looks like she'd rather be some place else. The woman's frown at the old priest's retreating back didn't bode well, but Harry had already gotten himself in too deep to turn away.

He hoped his smile reassured as much as he intended and did the only thing he could. He offered her his arm. Her glance at the watchers all around them passed so quickly Harry hoped no one noticed it. She took his arm with one hand, holding her son's in her other.

"Shall I show you the cathedral, corporal?" she asked.

"Harry," he said in a faux whisper, bringing an amused smile to her face.

They climbed the ancient steps, and she paused on the top to point out the medieval carvings still visible between the sandbags and flickering in the candlelight. The people of Amiens left the mark of their professions and a record of their lives in stone of the great entranceway centuries before. Winemakers, beekeepers, family groups, and sheepherders covered the lower walls, all long gone and yet somehow present in the people enjoying the Christmas market.

He took a step back and looked up. Above them, saints and

kings, arrayed in proper order, looked down sternly. Above them all, Christ sat upon a throne, his hands extended in front of him.

"Mercy or judgment?" Harry wondered with a frisson of discomfort.

"Do you see?" she asked, pointing. "The saved on one side, the damned on the other? Saint Michel holds the scale, but the devil, he tries to cheat."

The devil certainly had his way along the Somme these past months. Harry wondered if she felt the same.

She hurried them inside.

Harry vaguely recalled hearing that Amiens was the tallest of the gothic cathedrals. Bathed in candlelight, he could see that the stone, rippling like water, soared upward only to disappear, the ceiling lost in darkness. Here and there candles lit the gloom.

"Better to see it in daylight," Rosemarie told him, her voice echoing in the cavernous building.

Marcel latched on to his mother's leg. She bent to pick him up, but Harry reached for him. After a moment's hesitation, she let him take the boy. Neither mother nor son objected, and Harry liked the feel of the warm little body on his shoulder.

Walking down the north aisle behind her, Harry's attention fixated on the animated form of the woman who gestured toward various statues rather than on the art itself. She became more enthusiastic as they went, her obvious pride in the place overcoming the awkwardness she had displayed when the *abbé* left them together. She fascinated him as no statue or relic—even the reputed head of John the Baptist—could.

In one dark corner, they passed two lovers locked in embrace. She hurried past, only to encounter another couple in an even more amorous position several feet farther along. Harry turned the boy's head to his shoulder with a chuckle, and Rosemarie flashed him a stern look, one that didn't quite reach her dancing eyes.

She led him toward the center. A wall of sandbags like the

ones outside greeted them, so tall he couldn't make out the top in the gloom.

"What are we protecting here?" he asked.

"The Renaissance choir stalls are in there, but they protect the polychrome, I think."

"Polychrome?"

"Carvings of the lives of Saints John the Baptist and Firmin painted in bright colors. *Abbé* taught me they are from the fifteenth century—not so old as the cathedral but quite ancient nonetheless. They are among the great treasures."

"Firmin? I don't know that name," he said.

"A Roman who came here to be bishop and was martyred."

"Came here and was killed? He has a lot of company," Harry spat without thinking.

Her stricken face made his heart sink.

"I'm sorry, Rosemarie. Tonight is a night to forget all that."

Her eyelids fluttered. *Blinking back tears?*

"I think it's time we got this boy his sweet cake," Harry said, bringing a sad smile to her face.

In the square, they found food booths, and Harry bought cakes for all three of them from a sour-faced woman who glowered at Rosemarie but took his coin readily enough. Marcel devoured the sweet, but Rosemarie, he noticed, took a nibble and put the rest in her pouch.

"For later," she said.

For Marcel, he thought, remembering her empty larder.

"We should try another to compare. Perhaps we'll like it better," he said, glaring at the unpleasant vendor as he led them to another table. He pronounced the second so superior that he insisted on buying a loaf of bread and then demanded that Rosemarie take it because he "forgot" he had no place to store it.

When he led them to a third, she objected.

"Enough," she hissed. "People will think you are keeping me."

He opened his mouth to disagree, but her determination and his own good sense made him see the wisdom.

"Look, Marcel," Rosemarie said. "The puppets are back."

Harry watched the boy—on his mother's hip now and with the remains of his second sweet cake in his hand—laugh at the antics of Guignol. It settled a sort of peace deep in his soul. *If I'm not careful, I'll start to crave this.*

When the show ended, Marcel licked the last of his treat from his fingers, and Rosemarie announced she had to get the boy home.

Harry realized then it was too late to be careful; he already craved the company of this woman and her son. The thought of war and his place in it left him desperate to remain.

"I'm sorry, Harry. We can't stay longer. He will be asleep as soon as I push away from the quay as it is. Will you come for your Bible?"

He saw hope in her eyes or convinced himself he did.

"I'm afraid I can't now. *Abbé* Desjardin has to return me to Querrieu at sunup tomorrow. They'll have me shipped back to my platoon before I can breathe. I—" *You'll what, Harry? You can't promise anything. You belong to the Canadian Expeditionary Force, body and soul.*

"I'll try to come back. To fetch it."

She dropped her eyes. He hoped he didn't mistake the disappointment in her eyes.

"Good night, Harry. Thank you for the sweets," she said.

He watched her walk toward the river until she disappeared into the crowd, afraid to follow for fear he would beg her to take him with her. Harry stood in the square, bereft and alone, for a long while.

He gradually drifted toward the fringes and had begun to walk toward the neat little *auberge* the priest had recommended when two gaudily made-up women sidled up to him. One rubbed up against his left side while the other made a show of smoothing his lapels while she spouted a practiced patter about lonely soldiers and brave "*Anglais*."

Harry shook his left shoulder to free himself and took a step away. "You mistake me, madam," Harry said. "I am not English but Canadian. I'm sorry to inform you that, lovely though you may be, yours is not the company I seek."

The eyes of the one who had spoken to him widened at his perfect French. "Not now, but perhaps later?" she asked with a lift of her voice.

She reached into a small purse and pulled out a crumbled piece of paper and pressed it into his hand. Harry glanced down at the address of a house on the Rue St. Roch. *This is probably the one McNaughton salivated over.* He shook his head.

The bolder of the two gave a shrug that managed to convey both acceptance and a hint of seduction as if to say, "Your loss, soldier."

The two of them wandered back into the darkness, a sashay of the hip telling him they knew he watched.

Already heated from two hours in the company of Rosemarie Legrand, the sight sent his arousal galloping higher in spite of his efforts to ignore it. He needed something to numb his aching soul and cool his unruly body.

His preferred whisky being generally in short supply, he set out in search of wine. Food shortages there may be, but the French kept wine shipments to Picardy coming. Harry had rarely touched the stuff before the war, but he had drunk it in France on the rare occasion he was free from the army's clutches. He found a back alley bar where the wine was cheap and downed a bottle. When it failed to subdue his urgent yearnings and thoughts of the girls in that house on Rue St. Roch started to sound more attractive, he downed another. A free-spending soldier finds many friends in a bar willing to laugh, sing, and drink his wine. He ordered more.

Harry fell fully clothed into bed long after midnight and lay comatose until the reverend father shook him awake in the morning. Harry wasn't sure who appeared more disgusted when he stumbled downstairs, the priest or the innkeeper. Neither spoke.

Overindulgence and bobbing boats do not mix well. Harry swallowed repeatedly and kept his eyes closed, trying to suppress his stomach's threatened rebellion while *Abbé* Desjardin moved his little boat against the current, heading upstream toward British headquarters.

The old man pulled the boat into a sheltered pool near the shore and anchored it with a sigh. "You'll feel better if you empty the filth from your belly," he said.

Harry obliged, retching until he thought his stomach lining would fall into the water.

"Sorry," he mumbled, falling back into his seat.

"Did it help?"

"Retching?"

"No. The drinking."

"Not one bit. The war still waits." He held his stomach to calm it.

The priest considered his words for a few moments. "This need to drown your pain, it had nothing to do with Rosemarie Legrand?" Black eyes looked deep into his as if they already saw the truth.

"Perhaps. Are men in hell happier for a glimpse of heaven?"

The piercing eyes gentled. "Perhaps not," the old man said, "but a store of memories might be medicinal in coming months. Will you come back?"

Will I? He turned around to face forward, and the priest poled the boat out of the shallows, seemingly content to allow him his silence.

"How did you arrange my leave?" Harry asked at last, giving voice to a sudden insight.

"Prayer," the priest said. Several moments later, he added, "And Colonel Sutherland in the logistics office has become a friend. I suggested he had a pressing need for someone who could translate requests from villagers."

"Don't meddle, old man. Even if they use me, I'll end up back in the trenches. Visits to Rosemarie Legrand would be futile in any case. The war is no closer to an end than it was two years ago."

"Despair can be deadly in a soldier, corporal. You must hold on to hope. We all need hope, but to you, it can be life or death," the priest said.

Life or death. He thought of the feel of the toddler on his shoulder and the colors of *les hortillonnages. Life indeed.*

The sound of the pole propelling them forward filled several minutes.

"So will you come back?" the old man asked softly. He didn't appear discomforted by the long silence that followed.

"If I have a chance to come, I won't be able to stay away," Harry murmured, keeping his back to the priest.

"Then I will pray you have a chance," the old man said softly.

SLEET PINGED against the little window over Rosemarie's sink long after sundown on Christmas Eve. There would be no snow, and she would have no company this night. She turned to watch her son playing with a tiny figure of a sheep she had formed out of straw to add to their crèche.

A blast of wind sent an icy draft against the back of her neck. Their cottage, like most of those in *les hortillonnages,* was never built to withstand winter winds. It had been her father's summer garden, a place of refuge from the city in hot weather. *Poor Papa, long gone now.* He used the tiny woodstove on the occasional cool evening. Rosemarie needed it constantly as the weather turned nasty.

Marcel sat on a rug protected from the stove by their kitchen table, overturned to serve as a barricade while she cleaned their dishes. Their aging hens had presented her with extra eggs as a Christmas gift, and he had eaten his enthusiastically. Another went into a tiny cake. She had no butter for it, but she had saved her last bit of sugar in anticipation. Marcel loved it.

The boy seemed to respect the barricade, but she knew better than to turn away for long. She suspected he would spend much of the winter tied to his chair to protect him from both falls and the hot stove.

The little boy waved the sheep at her. "Sheep," he said, pulling himself to his feet and pointing to the crèche Rosemarie had arranged on a trunk in the far corner.

The figures were plain; her father had carved them from dark wood and left them unpainted, but they were dear to Rosemarie. She knelt with Marcel in front of it, and he immediately pointed to the mother. Naming the figures had become a favorite game.

"Mar'," he said.

"Yes. Marie," Rosemarie told him. "And this?"

"'osif," he said.

So it went through the figures.

"am'l," he said, naming the kings' camel. He turned to the other side. "Sheep," he said, handing over the one in his hand. She put it at the feet of one of the shepherds. He pointed to the little figure. "'arry," he said.

"Yes," she whispered. "Harry."

She had given up trying to get him to say shepherd. The straw sheep had been his Christmas gift, presented after supper. That and warm mittens were all she had to give. The boy seemed happy enough, and his joy was her gift.

"Shall we tell the story?" she asked.

He nodded solemnly and raised his arms to be carried.

She righted the table with one hand while holding Marcel on her other hip, brought the lantern to the table, and removed Harry's Bible from the windowsill. Rosemarie couldn't read

English, but that didn't matter. An artist blessed this edition with ink drawings, and Rosemarie knew the stories that went with each. The stories and the drawings together enchanted her son. She snuggled Marcel close and pulled the Bible over, opening it to Luke. A series of drawings preceded the gospel.

"Look at the angels, Marcel. Tonight is a night for angels."

"Sheep."

"Yes, the angels are singing to the shepherds and their sheep," she told him. "When the Christ child was born, angels appeared to—"

Knocking on their door made her heart pound; she gasped and grabbed her son so tightly he yelped his indignation. She surged to her feet.

"Who is there?" she shouted through the wood, one hand on her heart.

"Pere Noel," a familiar voice replied.

An angel.

CHAPTER 6

Rosemarie Legrand would never turn away a stranger. Harry knew that. He also knew the distance between welcome guest and tolerated intruder. He prayed he might be the former. If not his poor self, perhaps the bundles he carried might be truly welcome.

If he could have warned her, he would have, but it took him until late the previous night to convince the captain that holiday greetings in French were just the thing to deliver to allied head-quarters, something to ingratiate the captain with the brass hats, especially since it would include a bottle of wine Harry smuggled back from Amiens.

Perhaps "convinced" is less than accurate, Harry. You wore the man down.

The captain's last words were "Get yourself back here by sundown Tuesday, or I'll have you up on charges. And, corporal, I hope that girl is worth it." *No fool he.*

Now, here he stood, hours after he intended, with only Christmas Day free before him. He pounded on the door.

"Who is there?" It sounded like a challenge, not a welcome.

He took a deep breath.

"Pere Noel," he replied, praying she saw it that way.

When the door swung open, Rosemarie peered out cautiously before a smile began at the edge of her luscious lips and spread slowly across her face to her eyes. He let out the breath he had been holding and grinned back. She didn't move but stood riveted to the spot, her smile growing.

"May I come in?" he asked at last, finally aware of the sleet against his cheeks.

"Oh, my! Yes."

He had never seen Rosemarie flustered before, and he found it utterly adorable.

Inside, they stood and grinned like fools until Marcel, who stood holding his mother's skirt, made them both laugh with a raised fist and a joyful shout, "'arry!"

"I couldn't send word. I'm sorry I—" he began.

"Take off your boots and sit," she said at the same time.

Harry noticed his grandmother's Bible open to the angels when he put his sack on the table and sat to do as she told him.

"I couldn't get transport until almost noon," he told her.

"It is Christmas Eve. People have other things to do."

"Besides transporting lonely soldiers? Yes. Then headquarters delayed me. Every man there seemed determined to greet anyone who came in the door."

The forced holiday cheer depressed him, especially when he had feared he wouldn't make it to *les hortillonnages.*

"I had to share their wine," he went on, "though it looked to me like they had already emptied a few before I got there. But wait—"

He stepped outside and picked up his second bundle, an armload of dead branches tied with string. "For the fire," he said, closing the door behind him and handing her the fuel before she could object. He tossed his boots toward the door and sat up to see her staring back at him as if she was trying to memorize his features. Heat crept up until he feared his neck and chin—if not his entire face—must be rosy.

Rosemarie broke eye contact and leaned over to pick up the little boy. "Thank you for the wood, but what is this Pere Noel nonsense?" she asked.

"I met him along the way." Harry looked at Marcel with a smile. "He seemed rather busy, so I offered to deliver something for Marcel." He rummaged in his sack and pulled out a small package wrapped in waxed paper rescued from the cook-tent trash.

Marcel's eyes lit up.

Rosemarie put her son on a chair and belted him safely while he reached for the package. At first, he seemed content to examine the paper and string, but when Harry opened one end, he quickly tore into it and squealed with delight to uncover a *barque à cornet* the size of a man's hand. The boy's eyes danced.

"Bak," he said, holding it up.

Harry reached in and pulled out another package, causing the little one's eyebrows to fly toward his hairline. This time, he tore off the paper immediately but looked puzzled by the box inside. Harry had a moment of regret about the battered box from a soldier's tea, but the boy's delight with his gift banished such thoughts. He helped the tiny hands open the box to reveal a little boatman and his pole and oar, carved from the same wood as the boat. Marcel immediately put the man into his *barque* and the pole in his hand. The man had taken Harry a bit longer to carve than the boat, and Martens had helped with the oar.

"Bak," Marcel repeated, smiling before pushing the boat along the table.

"Thank Harry, Marcel," Rosemarie said, her eyes suspiciously wet.

"'arry!" the boy said, waving the boat and then putting it all back together to sail along the table again.

"The rest is for you," Harry said.

Rosemarie eyed the sack, put out a hand, and pulled it back

as if she feared getting burned. She glanced up at Harry and back down again.

"It is little enough," Harry said. "Just some things I was able to collect since I saw you three weeks ago."

"Collect?" she asked, looking at him.

"Here and there." He shrugged. "I did a few favors."

Few? Martens' emergency rations alone cost me latrine duty twice.

When she still hesitated, he upended the sack, and boxes spilled out onto the table. He had managed to collect four boxes of tea, a half-dozen boxes of biscuits, and three each of salt and sugar.

"They make us carry 'iron rations' with us. We're to save them for emergencies and eat what they send from the cook tents, except we don't always use them. These are mine and Martens' and another man's," he told her.

That other one a miracle.

McNaughton had walked up to him two days before and dropped his ration in Harry's lap. The sergeant didn't meet his eyes and just said, "Orders are we keep those with us, corporal. I wouldn't want to see one of my men give them away. I'd have to write him up." He had emphasized the word "see," and Harry tossed the rations in with the rest of his hoard.

Rosemarie wasn't looking at biscuits or tea. She stared at the real treasures. Each of the ration packages had a tin of corned beef. Four of them now lay across her table along with three large tins of vegetables. A cotton sack held turnip flour salvaged from the cook crew after he helped them clean up. The fourth beef and the vegetables cost Harry a pair of wool socks he would miss desperately during the winter, but not as badly as Rosemarie and Marcel would miss meals.

It took some coaxing, but Harry helped her store the hoard away with her meager supplies. When he withdrew his hand from putting the tins of beef on a shelf, she grabbed it and kissed his knuckles without a word, swallowing hard and blinking back tears. He wasn't sure if the kiss or the tears made his knees so weak he had to sit.

She insisted on brewing some of the tea, while Harry played with Marcel. When she brought it, he half expected the army biscuits, but she served the remains of a small cake instead.

"Our Christmas Cake," she said. "I was going to save some for morning."

Harry's instinct was to give his share to the boy. *Eat it, you fool. Don't insult her hospitality.*

As if she read his mind, she said, "You've given us too much. I have nothing for you."

He put down his cup. "You've opened your home to me. You let me enjoy your son. You have no idea how much this means after months of moldy tents and muddy trenches." *And blood and death.* "It is a bigger gift than you can imagine. Besides," he went on with a twinkle in his eye, popping the last bite of cake into his mouth, "you shared your heavenly dessert."

She relaxed, her joy unfolding like a flower in front of him, and his heart opened wide to let her in. They sat in perfect contentment, listening to the little boy's chatter.

Harry reached over a while later and touched the Bible. "You were reading?" he asked.

"In English? No. We look at pictures, and I tell him the stories."

"My grandmother insisted I bring it. I'm glad she did."

Memories of another kitchen, a bigger one with an overflowing larder and the smell of cinnamon and nutmeg emanating from the oven, filled him. The farm in Saskatchewan had always been a place of safety and peace to him, far from his father's house in Regina where there were rules to keep and standards to be measured by.

I'll take Rosemarie and Marcel there some day. Grandma will like that. The thought came unbidden, but it lodged itself deep within him. He shook his head to clear it.

"Shall we tell stories?" he asked.

Rosemarie pulled Marcel into her lap and pointed to a picture of angels. She began to tell the story of the shepherds, and Harry realized he had interrupted it with his arrival. Her soft voice burrowed deep in his soul, places that hadn't been reached in many years.

Marcel fell asleep to the sound of his mother's voice, as boys inevitably do.

"Let me put him to bed," she murmured. "I'll be but a moment."

Harry pulled the Bible over. Most of the pages were warped from water damage, and some were stained from the mud, but it felt familiar all the same. It never failed to fill him with thoughts of home. *I will take them there.*

Foolish that. You don't know what tomorrow will bring, or when this war will end.

Rosemarie returned, looking as flustered as she had when she found him at her door. "He's asleep," she said as if he didn't know it.

"Rosemarie, may I stay tonight?" His gaze never left hers.

She put up both hands as if to defend herself and blushed.

Before she could speak, he rushed on. "I mean no disrespect. I will sleep on the floor by the stove. Soldiers are used to sleeping rough."

Her body relaxed, and she blinked.

He continued, "I rented my own boat this time. I can leave, but it's dark, and I—" He sighed. "I really want to spend Christmas here."

She stepped closer then. "I want it, too," she whispered.

Her face was inches from his. She reached up a hand to push back his hair. He leaned in to smell her scent, all roses and woman.

Before he could close the distance for a kiss, she put a hand on his chest. "You will sleep on the floor. By the stove," she said tartly, one brow raised.

"Yes, ma'am," he said, smiling.

He took her mouth gently. At her eager response, passion flared, and his kiss deepened before moving to her neck and the warm spot under her ear. The sound of her moan almost undid him.

An urge to ask her to marry him almost drove him to foolish declarations. *Not now. Not yet. But perhaps someday. When all this is over, I will take her home. Let tomorrow bring what it brings. For now, this kiss will have to be enough.*

He lifted her, carried her to her rocker, enfolded her in his arms, and began to kiss her in earnest.

PART II

SHEPHERDS IN THE FIELD

CHAPTER 7

March, 1917
Les Hortillonnages

Planting peas and cabbage fed Rosemarie's hope; early crops always did. Soon enough food would be abundant again, perhaps enough to sell in Amiens. She knelt in her garden, pulled weeds, and let the sun warm her back, relieved by useful work and delighted Marcel could play outside. Harry's infrequent visits livened a winter that had otherwise been dark and miserable, but they stopped soon enough, and she had only her garden to lift her spirits. Christmas felt like a lifetime ago, and her heart tightened in her chest at the memory.

Late winter brought a resumption of full-scale fighting across northern France, not that it had ever stopped, and as Harry's visits stopped and letters stretched ever farther apart, she came to believe her time with him would dwindle into a warm memory and little more.

Will that be all we have of him? That and the memory of his gentle hands?

A call from the river intruded on her morose thoughts. "Rosemarie, I bring news," *Abbé* Desjardin called, poling his boat up to her dock. He tied up the *barque* and jumped out with the agility of a much younger man. Rosemarie stood and brushed her hands together. She smiled when Marcel looked up from his play to grin at the priest who ruffled his hair.

The sight of a folded paper in the abbé's hand reignited her fear. "From Harry?" she asked, wiping her hands on her apron and reaching for it.

"For certain, though the harried-looking private who brought it said only 'from the corporal' before he rushed out. What other corporal do we know?"

"He must have been in a hurry," she said, wiping her hands on her apron. The British military mail had proven unreliable when the destination was other than England or empire.

While neatly folded, the paper looked crumpled as if it had been grasped too tightly in someone's hand. Her name had been written across one fold with the *abbé*'s direction. She flipped it open and found a message, brief and hurried, in Harry's familiar scrawl strewn across the page. She read over and over until the words blurred.

We are moving again. Will write when I can. Harry.

"Leaving?" *Abbé* Desjardin's sympathetic expression almost undermined Rosemarie's determination not to turn into one of those weeping women who cling to soldier's coat tails. If the men could march into German guns, she could show courage. "Yes. Moving at least." She couldn't resist one lament. "He might have added something personal."

"Words of undying love?"

Rosemarie felt her cheeks heat. "At least. And in rhyming verse."

The abbé's chuckle rewarded her lame attempt at humor. "Not a particularly manly notion."

"No," she agreed. "Harry's poetry doesn't stoop to drivel in any case." Once, in better days, he left one for her, in French and in English.

"At least you know he thought of you when the army ordered him north."

"North? Into Belgium?"

"Arras at least. We hear rumors of fierce fighting."

Fierce. Deadly. Her eyes prickled again.

"Listen Rosemarie. You know he thought of you."

She nodded, unable to speak. *There is no date. How long ago did he leave?*

"You will see him again, my dear. You must have hope."

Will I? She glanced down at the paper, crushed now in her clenched fist. Hours later, with the *abbé* fed and gone, and Marcel tucked in bed, she spread the note on her little table and smoothed out the creases and tucked it in Harry's Bible with the poem.

The temptation to hug the book to herself as if it were Harry himself shook her. *He gave you strength when you needed it, Rosemarie. He deserves better than someone who collapses in the face of fear.* She carried the Bible upstairs instead, put it in her little chest, the painted one her father had given her when she left home, and turned the key in the lock.

EVERLASTING RAIN, *rain and darkness,* Harry thought. *God, I hate March.*

He sat next to Sergeant McNaughton in the shelter of a *souterrain*—one of the underground caverns carved by generations of Frenchmen into the chalky soil—gazed out the opening across open fields at an uplifted ridge of rock that loomed in the distance. Since the Somme and Harry's Christmas interlude, the two men had become friends, moving beyond rank and formality.

Harry trusted Mac, as he'd been given leave to call him, with his life.

From their vantage point they couldn't make out the Germans' barbed wire and machine gun bunkers through the mist and rain, much less the entrenchments, but they knew they were up there. Waiting.

"You haven't said much, Harry," Mac said.

"About what?"

"The captain's briefing."

Harry snorted.

"Yep," Mac drawled. "That's about it."

The silence between them echoed how much the British commanders cared what a corporal—a Canadian one at that—thought of their plans.

"Could be worse," Mac said at last.

"How?"

"This cave they billeted us in is less muddy than the damned trenches along the Somme. Chalk they say."

"That the best you've got?"

"We don't have to follow the Brits."

"True enough, that," Harry agreed. All four Canadian divisions would be in this one shoulder to shoulder. They would fight and die together.

"What are you going to tell your squad?"

"Me? You're senior in the platoon," Harry said.

"Don't tell Lieutenant Harvey that."

"Harvey is hiding again. He won't tell the platoon anything."

"Squad level, the captain said. They want us maneuvering at the squad level. Climb that damned ridge any way we can. We drill at the squad level again tonight."

That was another thing, charging in the dark at dummy targets, working through the night alongside engineers to expand tunnels and subways. "I feel some sodding owl. We've hardly seen daylight in a month," Harry spat.

"Keeps the Huns guessing what we're up to," Mac replied. "And you didn't answer. You need to talk to your squad. It's you they have to follow, not Harvey. Captain says we're to stick together, and a ten-man squad is easier to keep track of than a company, easier to move as needed."

Harvey's platoon had three squads. McNaughton's squad had twelve men and Wilbur Jones's, nine. As corporal, Harry led ten men. The Canadian officers' insistence on flexibility at the squad level surprised him.

"Makes sense though, the flexible part. Try to hold a rigid line and we all go down," Harry mused.

Mac spat. "At least we don't have to pretend to wait for Harvey to lead."

Harry felt a rumble of laughter bubble up, irrational and inappropriate. Soon he was doubled over and choking out his words. "There is that. Poor Harvey couldn't lead sheep to a field full of grass." He lay flat after that, panting until he recovered, and pushed himself up onto an elbow. "How do you plan to keep Walker moving forward?" he asked.

"You mean 'King and Empire' won't work?" Mac didn't actually expect an answer. "Assuming he hasn't shot himself in the foot between now and then, I may just put myself at the blighter's back, gun in hand."

"I'm glad he's in your squad, not mine. The three new men they gave me will be ready to throw themselves at German guns. I only hope they remember how to user theirs," Harry said. "I'll have to put them in between Martens and some of the other senior men."

"What do you plan to tell them?" Mac asked again.

"What can I? The British brass wants Vimy Ridge, but they aren't sure the benighted Canadians can do it. We plan to prove them wrong. That ridge and the guns on it are ours." *That and keep your head down, stick close together, and pray.*

"Good man. You know they trust you."

Harry fought back bile rising in his throat. *Bad enough to charge uphill into gunfire; worse to lead other men to it.*

"All we have is each other, Harry. If not you, then who?" Mac murmured, studying his face.

Who indeed. He closed his eyes and tried to conjure up Rosemarie in his mind, to let the memory of her snuggled up in his arms heal his soul, but the image flickered, pushed aside by others that intruded, the faces of Martens, Willard, and the others in his squad and the sheer bulk of Vimy Ridge looming in front of him.

CHAPTER 8

March gave way to April with no word from Harry; Rosemarie stopped waiting for a letter. At least she told herself she did. A blessing came her way that month, from an unexpected source. The allied armies' never-ending need for uniforms caused the high command to open a workshop in Amiens, with jobs for women. A note arrived from a clerk in the logistics and supply division offering her work.

With the promise of pay and nothing to lose, she took Marcel to the workshop in response, hoping a mother with a child could bring piecework home. She hefted him onto her hip and waited behind one other woman. Approaching three years in age, the boy's growth would quickly make that feat impossible. The place vibrated with energy. Clerks bustled this way and that. Carts piled high with packages wheeled in, and others wheeled out.

Materials in. Uniforms out, she guessed. *Or damaged clothing in; repaired out, perhaps.*

"Can you operate a sewing machine?" The hiring clerk's demand brought her back from her abstraction.

"Of course, but—"

"Three francs a week. Can you start today?" the obviously harassed clerk replied.

Her head raced at the thought of what she could do for Marcel with hard currency. *Marcel!* She addressed her biggest concern. "I have a little one and—"

"Marta manages 'em. Lunch for the nipper is included."

She'd have done it just to give Marcel lunch, but they offered her coin as well. "I'm here now," she replied, eager to start.

In short order she found herself in a room lined with sewing machines, humming along under the hands of a score of women. She had been correct on both counts. There were piles of tunics and trousers to repair; there were patterns and material to make new ones. A matron assigned Rosemarie to repair detail.

The sun hung low in the sky by the time she seated Marcel in her *barque* and started for home. He prattled enthusiastically about a day spent playing with new friends. Her day had been somewhat less stellar but successful nonetheless. She had learned three things.

Not every woman in Amiens listened to her sister-in-law, Sabine, or even liked her. Most of her coworkers surprised her with their congenial openness, happy to let her work speak for itself. A few raised eyebrows told her that her relationship with a Canadian soldier hadn't gone unnoticed, but that seemed counted in her favor.

She also discovered that Colonel Sutherland, the *abbé*'s friend, oversaw the entire logistics and supply division, which did much to explain her recruitment.

One final piece of news sounded best of all. US President Woodrow Wilson's war cabinet had voted unanimously in favor of declaring war on Germany. Corporal Butler, the clerk who oversaw the shop, had made the announcement mid-morning. It hadn't happened yet, but it brought American involvement a giant step closer. The women in the tailoring shop agreed that would shorten the war; they agreed they should all pray it happened soon.

For now, she had work to do, busy hands, and distractions.

Marcel went happily along the next day, and Rosemarie took up her seat again. Each piece of clothing came with a name and a number. *Johnson, II-2-4-2-3,* she read.

"What do the numbers mean?" she asked the woman next to her.

"Don't know. Where they are I guess," Marcellina, the woman who worked next to her said.

"Unit number," the matron clarified, handing her a tunic with the sleeve missing.

"Its an odd number," she replied the next time she went by.

"Not so odd." The matron pointed a finger and traced from number to number. "Corps, division, brigade, company, platoon. Sometimes battery. Fliers are different." She didn't elaborate.

From that moment on, Rosemarie read every name, tried to picture a face for each, and hoped to see "Wheatly" on a repair tag. *A repair would mean he's alive, wouldn't it?* The numbers might tell her where he was. Watching and hoping gave her a reason to work faster.

AN OIL LAMP cast shadows on the walls of the little room carved into chalk where Harry tried to pound some sense into the men circled around him.

"Dark as a coal pit again today," Laporte groused into a lull.

Did he read my mind? Harry wondered. *Mid-afternoon and dark as night. Again.*

The cocky kid smirked at a man across the table from him. "Black as Willard."

Willard's dark skin made him a target of insolent louts like Laporte too many times. Once would have been too much for Harry, but Willard never rose to the bait. Twice Laporte's size and half again his age, Willard never lost his composure, earning Harry's respect and gratitude.

"Good day for it, though," Willard said before Harry could intervene, his deep voice rumbling up from his chest.

"How's that?" Martens asked.

"Good Friday, isn't it?" Willard replied.

"So it is," Laporte replied, "As good a day as any to talk about killing."

Killing. Looking at the faces of men he would send up the ridge, Harry wondered, sick at heart, which ones would not come down. It brought him back to weapons and tactics.

"Pay attention Laporte," Harry demanded. "When the time comes, stay alert, and you'll stay alive." Laporte's insolent expression didn't reassure him.

"When do we attack, Corporal?" Sullivan asked. "Waiting around makes me crazy." A bit of Irish echoed in the lad's voice; Harry suspected his folks weren't long off the boat. Skinny and freckled as he was, no one in the squad believed he was eighteen, as he had claimed when he enlisted. Harry would be surprised if the kid was a day over fifteen. Only a green recruit thought the waiting worse than getting shot at. Harry caught Michaels's knowing frown. Sullivan made Michaels look old and wise; perhaps he was. War had toughened him.

"Soon enough," Harry replied. He briefly reviewed what they already knew about managing their weapons on the run. Sullivan nodded, finding Harry's every word a pearl of wisdom; the veterans all looked as if their minds had wandered off, bored with the incessant review; and Laporte continued to smirk in his way that implied he found Harry unbearably stupid. "And when I say down, you all duck. I want heads down," Harry concluded.

"How dumb do you think we are, Wheatly?" Laporte snarled, glancing at Guerin, the other new recruit.

Harry looked directly at Sullivan. "Pay attention if you want to stay alive. The first time someone shoots at you your instinct will be to look for the source of the gunfire. Pop up, and they'll pick you off before you can blink."

His words left them silent. Even Laporte kept his mouth shut for once.

"So we go up together. We live and die together. We can't be at each other's throats." Solemn nods met that. "I want each of you new recruits attached to a more-veteran buddy. Guerin, you march next to Willard. Trottier, stay by Michaels. Sullivan, you stick with me."

He hesitated a moment, long enough for Martens to break in. "I'll double with Laporte. Smart as he is, I'll feel so much safer." He strung the word "so" out several syllables long, bringing laughter from his fellows. Laporte bristled.

"Pay attention to Martens, Laporte," Harry ordered. "No one knows everything, no one can do everything. Together you have a better chance of getting back down that ridge with all your body parts. Understood?"

Harry thought for a moment that the cocky Quebecer would give him more grief, but Laporte shot Martens a sullen look and seemed to think better of it. "Understood," he spat.

Harry rose wearily, and the men filtered out. In the dim passageway, he encountered McNaughton.

"The lieutenant wants us." When their eyes met, Harry saw his thoughts reflected in Mac's. Harvey wouldn't summon them if he didn't have word from higher up. They trudged through the tunnels without speaking.

The lieutenant didn't disabuse them of their assumptions. The line of battle had been announced; the attack was imminent. As expected, the Canadian Third Division would attack the center of the German line, but they already knew all that. The real news, when it came, wasn't good. Their platoon, their entire company, would attack in the first wave.

Harvey stared at the dispatch without reading it. He began fidgeting with his papers, hands shaking, never looking up.

"Still on for Easter?" Mac asked.

"Monday, didn't I say? Frenchies asked to wait," Harvey

responded.

"Not till Monday? We don't have to fight on Easter at least," Mac said.

"Perhaps we can ask the cooks if they can color powdered eggs to celebrate our good fortune," Harry replied, rolling his eyes.

Harvey's head bobbed up, looking as if he couldn't decide whether Harry meant it.

"Any change to the platoon's orders—sir?" Harry asked curtly, twisting the word "sir" until he drew a frown from McNaughton.

"You know what to do," Harvey mumbled, looking back down.

Of course they did. He, Mac, and Jones had worked it out between them. Harry couldn't stop himself. "And where will you be—sir?" he demanded.

"I'll be right behind you," Harvey said, still staring down and waving his right hand dismissively.

Far, far, behind. Harry bit down on his lip to keep from saying it. He snapped off a salute that didn't quite stop short of derisive. "Yes, sir. Thank you sir," he snapped and spun on his heels, but before he and Mac could make their escape, a courier hurried down the corridor and slid into Harvey's quarters.

"They've done it," he shouted, waving a paper. "Captain Mitchell says to tell the men. America finally declared war on the Huns!"

Harvey grabbed the paper, hand shaking, an obscure emotion gleaming in his eyes. "About damned time they did their bit," he growled. "Will this do it, do you think? Will the Germans turn tail?"

"Not bloodly likely," Mac spat. "And a garbagy piece of paper isn't boots on the ground. We still have to climb that damned hill on Monday."

"But it's the end, isn't it?" Harvey whined.

Not now. Not soon, you damned fool. Harry shook his head.

CHAPTER 9

The sleet began before dawn on Easter Monday, and they moved out soon after, the wind blessedly at their back and sleet in the faces of their enemies. The series of planned explosions undermining gun emplacements and a furious artillery barrage cleared their way. Harry's squad made "the black line," their first objective, without any problem.

They hunkered down and waited for the corps to consolidate and move forward. Harry glanced at his watch; it had been just one hour since the attack began. It felt like an eternity.

"Piece of cake, Corporal," Sullivan grinned.

"Don't get comfortable," Harry replied. "We've a long road to go."

They moved up with the rest of the troops, Mac's squad to their left, and Jones to their right. Intermittent snow mixed with the sleet as the squads zigzagged forward. Harry's squad stuck together like glue. Trouble came before long; heavy fire from their right found them.

"Down!" The squad followed Harry into the shelter of a shell crater. Guerin hesitated a moment to spot the source of their troubles and toppled over into the crater with his fellows.

"Dead." Sullivan's voice shook with horror. Harry had to move quickly before panic destroyed the boy.

"You're not!" Harry shouted. "You listened to me. Listen now, and keep your head down." He pushed Sullivan's head between his knees and ignored the sound of retching. They all did, just as they ignored the gaping hole in Guerin's forehead.

Willard's swearing fouled the already suffocating smoky air. "I pulled his hand, but the damned fool—"

"Not your fault," Harry told him. He rolled Guerin to his side away from them. "We need to move on up."

Laporte put his helmet on a stick and lifted it. The ping of a bullet sent it tumbling to the other side of the crater. "How?" he demanded.

"Someone has to stop those bastards," Willard said. "I'll do it." He began to rise, chin down.

"Willard—" Harry began. The big man paused, and their eyes met. Harry could see not only determination, but confidence.

"I'll maneuver around. Give me fifteen minutes You lot sit tight." He was gone, darting to the left, before Harry could object.

"Poor dumb bastard," Laporte mumbled.

We don't have fifteen minutes, Harry thought. They had objectives to take. *Besides, I can't leave these men here with Guerin's body. They'll lose it entirely. I have to keep them moving.* He peered over the crater wall.

"We'll move out to the left. Stay hunched over. Between that row of craters, what's left of the bushes, and the smoke, they won't get a good enough look to pick us off."

"But Guerin—" Sullivan began.

"Leave him. Now." Harry led the way over the crater wall; every one of them followed in a closely packed unit. Snow began to mix with the sleet, lightly at first, but quickly intensifying. They climbed upward through blinding snow, deafened by the sound of artillery and explosions. One more off to their right sounded like a grenade. Gunfire flew around them. Harry couldn't be sure how much came from the nest that had pinned them down and how much came from elsewhere; he could only put one foot in front of the other, pleased that his men remained a tight unit. Once he thought he saw McNaughton through a break in snow and gun smoke, but he couldn't be certain.

When Harry slipped over an unfortunately placed rock, six men dropped to their knees next to him. He crawled up immediately, glancing back and forth. "You're doing fine men. Keep moving."

Steps later, a group of figures emerged from the swirling mist, heading directly toward them, the distinctive sloped outline of German helmets sending chills through Harry.

"Huns!" Sullivan screamed, raising his gun. Harry, catching sight of the tall man looming behind them, shoved it down just in time to keep him from shooting one of their own.

"Willard, thank God!" Harry cried. "What—" He stopped, dumbfounded. The frightened eyes of five German soldiers stared back him. Some appeared to have shrapnel wounds to arms and torso. One bled profusely from a cut over his left eye. They carried a large machine gun. Willard stood grimly behind them with his rifle aimed at their backs.

"Got em, Corporal," Willard said through clenched teeth. "Six more dead back uphill. Only took two grenades, and this lot begged to be taken."

"The gun?"

Willard shrugged. "I thought our boys could use it."

A bark of laughter rocked Harry while his mind raced. *That gun killed Guerin, but I can't waste energy on it or on tending five prisoners.* "Take them down until you find headquarters battery. They'll be glad for it."

Willard grinned. "Thought they might." He loped on down the hill, poking first one disheartened German and then another with his rifle to keep them moving.

Harry called after him. "Good luck!" Willard would need it.

Sliding on the now-snowy ground, they pushed forward to the "red line," their next objective, without further incident. Orders were to pause there before moving on to take the German positions beyond it. He sat on the rocky ground and took stock. Six men waited to hear what he had to say; ten had followed him up. With Guerin dead and Willard gone—escorting his prisoners —he should have eight. "Where the hell are Martens and Laporte?"

Six pairs of eyes scanned the ridge, some frantic, some frightened.

"Dunno. They were right next to me, and then the snow, and —" Trottier stumbled to a halt.

"Martens will take care of him, Corporal, he knows what he's doing," another one said, but it sounded like wishful thinking. *Damned screw up Laporte. He'll get us all killed.*

"Maybe they got lost in the snow," Sullivan said. *More wishful thinking.*

Harry's orders were to pause and rest the men until the order came down the line to move. *Could they be lost? Martens is too reliable to wander off and too brave to hang back. Unless he had to chase Laporte. Where the hell are they? Do I have time to hunt for them?*

He couldn't risk the others. "We stay together. If they're lost, they'll have to catch up on their own."

"Maybe they're with Sergeant McNaughton's men," Trottier suggested.

Harry could just make out Mac several yards away, leaning over one of his men. He shook his head. "He'd send them over if they turned up. They better have a good story when they catch up. Latrine duty will get really old otherwise." That brought nervous laughter.

Where the hell are they? Harry couldn't stay put; he reached a decision. *Command's been pushed to the squad level, hasn't it?*

"Trottier, You're in charge. If I'm not back when the signal comes to move, attach yourselves to Sergeant McNaughton's squad. I'm going after Martens and Laporte."

He didn't have to go far. Twenty yards down the slope he found Laporte cradling Martens' bleeding body. One glance at the empty eyes told Harry he was too late. Laporte watched him come.

"You said to stay together. I couldn't leave him here alone."

"He's gone, Laporte," Harry told him, hunkering down on his heels. Martens had been a friend; he choked back his own grief.

"No, he's here. I have him. He knocked me down and fell on me and he's, he's…"

Harry put a hand on the private's arm. "You can set him down, now. He's gone."

Shock rattled Laporte's body. He looked bewildered. "I don't understand. I didn't see anything. He just pushed me, and, and…"

"Leave him. The detail will take care later. Let's get you out of here," Harry soothed. If they were lucky and held enough of the ground, a burial detail might be able to retrieve the dead. He put one arm over Laporte's shoulder and helped him lay the dead man on the hard ground. Harry pulled Martens' eyelids closed with a shaking hand, crossed the dead man's arms across his chest, and, removing his extra cartridges and weapon, handed them to Laporte. "We'll mourn later," he said, as much to himself as to the shaken private. "Let's go now."

Laporte blinked at him in uncharacteristic silence without acknowledging the words, but he followed.

They reached the squad just as word came to move out. The squad members looked at Laporte and glanced behind him, looking for Martens. No one spoke. Harry took a deep breath and gestured them forward. *Enough, God. No more.* He had led ten men up; he would lead seven down—eight if Willard made it.

~

THE LOW RUMBLE of artillery that lay like a pall over Easter continued to echo across the Somme on Monday morning as Rosemarie pushed her *barque* to the quay at Amiens, sick at heart. At Easter Mass, *Abbé* Desjardin had prayed for the allied troops around Arras.

Arras has to be at least seventy kilometers away. Is Harry there? And how many guns must fire for us to feel the reverberations here? She wondered again how much the old man knew. She hadn't been able to ask him Sunday morning, surrounded by people as he was. She lifted Marcel from the boat and hurried down the quay, not daring to be late for work.

Work piled high that Monday, as it happened, and by the time she got to Marcel, the boy whined with fatigue and hunger. Distracted by her son, it took her several moments to realize why something felt off when they stepped out into the street. The rumbling had stopped; she began to run.

A priest stopped her when she hurried down the corridor of the chancellery. "May I help you, madam," he asked.

"I must see *Abbé* Desjardin!"

Marcel pulled on her hand. "I'm hungry, Maman," he whined, drawing a frown from the priest.

"Care for your child. The *abbé* does not care to be interrupted when conducting parish business."

What is the parish business if not comforting its people? She didn't give voice to the thought. "Please. I won't take long. Tell him Rosemarie Lagrand wishes a word."

The priest, surely younger than Rosemarie but made old in his pomposity, shook his head and held up a hand as if to prevent her from barging into the office, but before he could speak, the door opened.

"Rosemarie, what is it?" the *abbé* asked, opening the door wide so she might come in.

She slipped around the self-important priest without wasting so much as a smug glance at the man.

"Abbé, the guns have silenced!"

Her old friend smiled sadly and shut the door behind her. "Sit, sit. You look tired."

She did as he invited, and pulled Marcel into her lap. He latched a little hand onto her cheek and pulled her face toward himself. "I want to go home, Maman," he whispered.

"We will darling. Soon."

"Marcel, come see what is in my desk," *Abbé* Desjardin suggested. The little boy glanced up at his mother before he slipped to the floor and went to look at the old priest's meager supply of lemon drops, popping one in his mouth and earning a pat on the head from the old man.

"Now. You come about the guns?"

"It must be over. You hear things. What—" When it came down to it, she didn't know how to frame her fears.

"What have I heard? Of Harry, nothing, of course."

"Of course," she muttered.

"The quiet is a lull only. The British have surrounded Arras, and the French push from the east. Their first goal—to knock the Germans from Vimy Ridge north of Arras—began this morning, the beginning move of much more fighting."

Rosemarie nodded absently, staring at her hands. He had told her nothing. What she already knew, she didn't care about.

"One thing," he went on.

Something in his voice made her look up sharply. "What is it?"

"The Canadian Corps was assigned to take the brunt of the first action. They were ordered to take the Vimy Ridge, I believe."

Bile rose in her throat, and she felt the blood drain from her face. Marcel crawled back into her lap, and she pulled him close.

"Do we know for sure he is there?" she asked. "His message said—"

"A soldier can't tell you things like that Rosemarie." The *abbé* leaned closer. "But my sources told me the entire Canadian corps was moved north of Arras. You can assume that he is with them. Pray. All we can do is pray."

For two days Amiens felt, more than heard, the intermittent artillery barrages from the north. For two days Rosemarie prayed. On Thursday she left work dragging a heavy heart and a tired son. As she neared the cathedral square, a boy selling newspapers caught her eye.

"*La Crête de Vimy capturé*," he shouted.

The entire first page of *La Press de Picardie* echoed his words, "Vimy Ridge Captured, 5,816 Prisoners." She dug into her purse for a few sou to buy a copy. Headlines always gave only the good news. Casualties must have been high.

Two hours later with Marcel fed and content, she sipped her tea—weak from reuse but warm and comforting—and read the paper through. She found what she dreaded on page three, "Canadian losses high…" and slumped in her chair.

He's there. I know he's there. The fighting around Arras continues. It could go on for weeks. He won't be able to contact me. What if he is wounded? What if he is ill? What if—

Her fevered thoughts ran in circles even as she cleaned up, even as she put her son to bed, and even as she tried to pray.

I have to know. I'll go mad if I don't know. One thought emerged from her chaotic emotions. *I must find him. There has to be a way.*

Wagons traveled back and forth to the staging areas. If she could find her way onto one, she could go there.

CHAPTER 10

Wise fathers lock their daughters up when battle-hardened troops are given leave to stand down. The remains of a nameless village nestled below the ridge west of the Scarpe—one of many reduced to piles of debris and shell holes a few miles north of Arras—rocked with drunken men toasting king and empire, singing Canadian songs, and chasing the few women who hadn't fled and who dared to ply their trade on the streets and encampments a few days after Vimy Ridge.

If worse happened, Harry didn't want to know about it. His squad occupied the remains of a tavern under a makeshift canvas roof, in which the proprietor had miraculously produced bad wine and worse beer. They had been joined by some others, none of whom were in a hurry to let the troops outside know what they had found. Periodic rumbles reminded them that fighting continued along the Scarpe. On this night, at least, their brigade stood down.

Harry leaned his back into the remains of a stone wall, one eye on the six men he held some influence over, and watched them drink themselves into oblivion while hoping to keep them from the worst of their folly. He had his own horrors to drown.

Willard, older and wiser than the others, sat across the table and sipped his beer slowly. *Make that seven,* Harry thought. *You have seven—eight counting Michaels.* Willard had found them four days after he passed them on the ridge. By all reports he'd climbed back up and fought his way down the other side. Harry and Mac planned to browbeat Harvey into recommending him for commendation. Michaels made it down with the others, but was so badly wounded he'd been evacuated to the field hospital.

Vimy Ridge had been a spectacular victory—a *Canadian* victory, and the men had a right to their pride, but Harry knew the lull for what it was. If the British Third failed to capitalize on it, their success wouldn't matter. Fighting continued, and it was only a matter of time before they were pulled back in, if only to keep the Germans busy while the French broke through along the Aisne—that is *if* the French could break through.

Sullivan slipped beneath a table, snoring loudly. The boy would be sick as a dog come morning. Laporte had a hand up a barmaid's skirt, regaling her in French. From the looks of her face, he either was making a fool of himself or was a far sight funnier than Harry believed.

"Where are the damned French?" Trottier shouted over the din. "Thought they were 'sposed to push the Huns back on the east." He got more belligerent by the minute. "And the damned Brits are no better."

"Wait for it, Corporal," Willard murmured.

Harry didn't pretend to misunderstand; they didn't have to wait long. Trottier's table exploded forward, and so did his fists. Soon Harry's squad, the sleeping Sullivan excepted, stood back to back along with a few sympathetic Aussies holding off two squads of British Tommies and a few locals.

When it was over, Harry sported a black eye, Trottier reported to medics to have his dislocated shoulder reset, and the others gloated. Willard hefted Sullivan over his shoulder while Laporte used his Gallic charm to promise payment for the damage.

"Feel better, Corporal?" Willard asked, as they trudged back to their billet.

Do I? Harry thought he rather did. Beating up the British felt better than remembering Marten's face anyway. "Of course not," he said. "Can't go around pounding on our allies. Think of the punishment. They might make us go fight the Huns." His men grinned back.

Pain shot up Rosemarie's back when the wagon hit another rut. She squeezed her eyes shut, shifted her weight, and took a deep breath. Tucked into the back of the wagon, wedged between tightly bound bails of uniforms, she had little room to move. She could neither complain nor ask the driver to stop. He and another private sat up top. They had, she had been told, only one day to get to Arras and back. She had been allowed to accompany the delivery on sufferance, on condition she help unload at the distribution point and load damaged goods to return.

It had taken her two weeks to convince Corporal Butler to order the logistics clerk who managed deliveries to take her, and another to wait for a window in the fighting that enabled delivery. Miraculously, Butler asked only for a *Tarte à la Rhubarbe* in exchange for her pass, and Marcellina offered to take Marcel for one night. Now she bounced on the Amiens to Arras road and hoped it wasn't a wild goose chase or worse.

After several stops they pulled into Arras itself, dodging debris, pack trains, and parades of wounded soldiers. The devastation horrified her; it shouldn't have. She'd heard bombardment all month, and it wasn't the first time. Armies had fought their way through Arras in 1914 and back again. The current offense centered here. Still, the piles of rubble, skeletal roof beams open to the elements, and the blank stare of window frames devoid of glass made her stomach roil. The damage in Amiens had been slight by comparison, at least so far, for which she offered a swift prayer of thanks.

They passed the Place de la Gare, the railroad yard, its station leveled to the ground, and into the town square, where a company of soldiers stood at parade rest preparing to march out. The driver pulled into a side street and came to a stop next to a building missing its upper stories, but solid and intact below. Through the open windows she could see it for the warehouse it was, though she suspected it had once been a stately home.

Rosemarie hopped down and winced when her right knee gave way, grabbing the wagon to keep from falling. The two privates came round the back and began pulling bundles from the wagon bed. She reached up to help, ignoring the stares of the men who swarmed out of the temporary warehouse.

"No need," the driver told her, yanking down a bundle and handing it to one of the warehousemen.

"But I agreed to—"

"Plenty of willing hands here," he said, gesturing with a nod of his head, without pausing his work.

Before she could think what to say, the man winked at her. "Not likely you can find your man in this, but give it a try. Go on. You have an hour."

She turned to go.

The driver called after her. "Don't be late—and watch yourself. Stay on the main streets. City's full of lonely men. We don't have time to rescue foolish women."

She shuddered but didn't pause, heading directly back into the town square, only to skid to a stop. She had no idea where to start. She skirted the square, looking for some sign of an office or headquarters. She stumbled along until she encountered three men hurrying past her who appeared to be officers.

"Excuse me, Sir," she said. "Where are the Canadians?"

Her face burned at the way two of them looked her up and down and chuckled. "Damned Canadians think they can commandeer all the good ones," one said to the amusement of his fellow.

The third glared at his companions, but the expression he turned on Rosemarie wasn't any friendlier. "You don't belong here, Mademoiselle. Whoever you seek has rather more important things to do."

"I came with the delivery wagon from the Amiens uniform workshop," she explained. "I just want to see my friend."

"Friend?" One of the rude ones raised his brows. "Is that what they call it in France?"

The more proper officer ignored that jibe. "There are Canadian units scattered along the line north of here. Is your 'friend' in a headquarters battery?"

"No," she said, her voice barely a whisper.

"Then I can't help you. I suggest you go back to Amiens."

When they spun on their heels and left her, she turned slowly around, taking in the devastation on all sides. A line of men pushing wheeled stretchers, empty now, turned down a street in front of her heading, she assumed, to the front.

What if Harry is in the thick of it? What if he is wounded?

She reached out to one of the stretcher-bearers. "Excuse me, where is the hospital?"

"Biggest one is across the square down that street toward the big church." He pointed, and she thanked God for his information. It wasn't much of an idea, but at least she could reassure herself if she went to the wounded and didn't find him. She might be able to do a kindness at least. Anything else seemed futile.

She trudged in the direction the man pointed, keeping her eyes forward and refusing to acknowledge any man who spoke, jeered, or leered at her. With every step, she realized just how foolish her decision to come here had been. Harry could be anywhere in a ten-mile radius, one of tens of thousands of troops. Worse, she feared he was at the front, not behind the lines where she was.

She approached a building that flew a white flag emblazoned with a red cross, and sped up. Just as she passed a gaping doorway, however, a hand darted out and grabbed her arm. Before she could object, she felt herself pulled inside and crushed against a solid chest, and blinded by terror, she choked on her screams, kicking and flailing her arms blindly.

CHAPTER 11

After three years of it, Harry had become numb to devastation, just as he grit his teeth and endured the mud, the barren trees, and the land devoid of life. Only Rosemarie's island gave him peace, but he couldn't afford to think of it lest the longing for her bring him to his knees.

He trudged through Arras, hatless and dirty, and passed the empty shell of a church without seeing it. Once the sight would have ripped his heart. No longer. He had more important concerns—Chris Michaels made it down Vimy Ridge, but wounds left him shattered. Harry had leave to check on him.

He held the boy's hand for an hour and then helped him dictate a letter to his mother, a dishonest but kindly meant description of what he'd seen and done.

"Don't want to tell her I had to shoot that Hun in the face, Corporal. Okay if I just say I knocked him down with my rifle to keep him from getting Trottier?"

"Tell her what she needs to hear, Michaels. It's a kindness."

The boy nodded. "Saved Trottier, didn't I?"

"You did indeed. You're a hero."

The boy on the bed, the top half of his head swathed in bandages, smiled. "Told her my broken leg's getting me transferred to England. I think I won't tell her about my eyes until my sight comes back. She'll know my hand's gone, but there'll be time for that. I just want her to know I'm okay, and that I was at Vimy Ridge. It was something, wasn't it, Corporal?"

"Yes, something…" Harry murmured.

"It was something, Vimy Ridge, wasn't it?" the boy repeated. "Wait until I tell the boys at O'Dwyer's Pub. I'll have stories, won't I?"

"Yes you will. We all will," Harry said. *The myths will echo from Saint John's to Vancouver. And who will tell the truth of it? This truth,* he thought, looking at the broken figure in the bed in front of him. He didn't begrudge the men their stories; pride may be the one good thing they take home with them—the ones that make it home. At least Michaels would be out of it now.

The hospital offices were situated a few houses down in the first building intact enough for them. It lacked a door and window glass, but the walls held up, and the upper floor kept the rain out. Harry stopped in to check on Michaels' transfer; he needn't have. The paperwork was in order with ruthless British efficiency. Curtly dismissed, he had no reason to linger, and nothing else to do.

He walked down the dark corridor head bowed, lifted his chin when he came to the door, and blinked in the sunlight. The vision that greeted him, glowing in the sun, was the one that haunted his dreams, the one light of hope in this darkness.

I've begun to hallucinate. Now I see her on the street.

Even as he thought it, the vision of Rosemarie walked on past. Instinct driving him, he grabbed the vision's arm to pull it close, warm, alive, and real in his arms. When he crushed the woman to him, she began to scream and kick, and the officious little clerk came running down the hall.

"Corporal, recall yourself before we call the RMP!"

He loosened his grip, but held on to one hand. The vision had been so vivid that he couldn't let her go. "Rosemarie! Rosemarie? It is you, isn't it?"

At the sound of his voice, the woman stopped fighting. "Harry?" she whispered. "Oh God, Harry!" She threw her arms around his neck so hard he fell back against the wall, and he laughed into her kiss.

She covered his face with kisses, and soon she was laughing and crying at the same time. "You're alive. You're uninjured. I've been so afraid."

He kissed away her tears. "I'm well, I'm well," he soothed.

The clerk walked away in disgust. "Find a private place, won't you," he muttered.

They laughed as one, and Harry led her by the hand out into the street.

"Where can we go?" she asked. "I only have an hour. Less now."

Harry looked around at the avid stares they were drawing, and his mind raced, searching for somewhere private enough to kiss her senseless, to touch, to— Reality struck him. "What the devil are you doing here? You don't belong in the middle of this hell." He didn't stop walking, but pulled her along, still holding her hand firmly in his.

"I came with the uniform delivery." She skipped to keep up. "Harry, it's amazing. I'm working in the uniform workshop in Amiens. For the British. Can you believe it?"

Resentment, quickly squelched, twisted his features. He wanted Rosemarie unchanged, exactly as he remembered, on her island. "You're making money," he said, knowing he should be glad. His eyes scanned the street, looking for a quiet spot.

"Yes, and it helps very much."

As badly as he wished he had the right to send her allotment from his pay, he did not. "I'm glad. It will help you and Marcel. How is he?"

She chattered on about the little one as he continued to hurry them down the street, describing his time in care, how tall he'd grown, the things he'd learned—all experiences lost to Harry, losses that added to his grief. He pushed them aside.

He came to the shell of the old church, without being aware he'd led her there. It was as deserted as he remembered. He led her to a corner of the remaining walls where they were hidden from the street and pulled her to him. She opened eagerly to his kiss, and he deepened it, slipping into her mouth as gently as he could manage, but her hands threading his hair, cupping his cheek, caressing his rib cage drove him mad. He put one hand under her rounded bottom and pulled her up against him, the other hand lifting her skirt at the same time.

Moments later the sound of a platoon marching by brought him to his senses. The aftermath of battle made some men rutting beasts, but Harry wasn't one of them. He let her slide to her feet, keeping one arm around her waist, breathing heavily. "Rosemarie, you can't know what this does to me."

She smiled into his mouth and rubbed her hand along the ridge pressing the front of his trousers. "I have some idea," she murmured, punctuating her words with swift little kisses.

"Yes," he murmured, "but not now. Not here." His head spun, and his soul twisted in knots. He wanted her moaning in passion. He wanted her desperately—Rosemarie had become all he knew of life and goodness, sunlight and hope, in the darkness of war. But he wanted her someplace beautiful, nestled in his arms. He wanted her safe.

"I don't want you here," he murmured, his kisses along her neck and ear, making his words a lie. "Arras is ugly and dangerous."

"I had to come." She responded in kind. "I couldn't bear the worry."

"It isn't over, Rosemarie. I should be on my way back now. We're joining the front tomorrow." He cupped her cheek and stared into her eyes trying to make her understand. "I need you and Marcel to be safe. I don't want to see you in this hellhole—I want to imagine you at *les hortillonnages*. It's all that keeps me sane."

She stepped away from him, standing just in reach. "But I'm not safe. Don't you see? None of us are. I'm not a marble statue in a garden, Harry." Her eyes pleaded with him for understanding.

He stared back, knowing she was right. Amiens hadn't borne the damage Arras had, but the fight wasn't over. Rosemarie had shown herself to be tough and resilient, and he admired her for that. She would have to be; the war raged on, and he wouldn't be there to protect them. He reached over and tucked a lock of hair behind her ear.

"I know. You are strong and courageous," he said. *And I love you for it.*

"We have to have hope. Without it I would curl up and die," she told him.

"Never. Marcel needs you. I need you. When this is done—"

She stopped him with a hand over his mouth. "Do what you need to do, Harry. Marcel and I will wait. I don't need promises."

He kissed her then, long and tenderly, putting his promises into it. *This war will end, and I will come for you.* That belief kept him going. It had to be enough; it was all they had.

CHAPTER 12

As spring passed into summer, the utter sameness of Rosemarie's days blurred each week into the next. Five days a week she poled into Amiens to work. Saturdays she tended her garden while Marcel floated the *barque* Harry had given him in a barrel. She had one note from Harry, delivered by a circuitous route through the army mails by Corporal Butler who administered uniform orders.

"I had to search through the undelivered mail for someone. Saw your name," he said. "Overseas mail goes out first," he added with an apologetic shrug. "Local stuff sometimes sits, and I don't think they could make out the address."

She glanced at the scrawled attempt to address it to her cottage on the island and made a mental note to remind him to send mail through the *abbé* before thanking the man for his kindness and ripping into the short note inside. It was dated three weeks before.

"Bogged down at Arras. Again," it said and little more. The man who wished to write couldn't bring himself to tell her the truth of his days. At least he added, "I think of you daily," but not "love." Never love. She thought he might love her, but he had never said it; he certainly didn't commit it to paper. She blinked back memory of the destruction at Arras and revisited the feel of his body holding hers; the note went into the trunk with the others.

She replied to the address he had given her, with his rank and unit, carrying it to the military mail office by herself, just as she did every week. She had no idea if he got her descriptions of Marcel's antics, the garden's progress, or work, and she was running out of cheerful topics.

Word of the failure of the French at Aisne depressed everyone. The war rolled on, covering the same ground over and over, an endless churn of destruction to their north and east and tension on the streets of Amiens. The allies stretched like a wall above the city; they could only pray it held.

When American troops finally arrived in France at the end of June, word spread through the city—and the workshop—like wildfire. Hope flared as if the Americans were angels descended from the heavens. Rosemarie allowed herself to hope with the others, although one of the clerks muttered darkly about raw troops and warm bodies.

Another note arrived, this time via the *abbé* and only a week behind, but it said as little as the last. The weather, he said, continued to be foul. He continued to miss her. Rumors flew that the British were pushing north toward Belgium, pressing around Lille, but he said nothing about that; she knew the censors would have blacked it out if he had. She had no idea whether he was in Belgium or France.

Images of Arras haunted her. All France would be a similar wasteland if the war went on much longer, and Harry, wherever he was, fought for his life.

She left work in mid-July and bustled through the cathedral square on a sunny afternoon where the old church still hunkered behind its wall of sandbags. Marcel skipped along next to her, healthier and well fed, as he had not been the year before. At three, he grew taller daily. Several people huddled around the newspaper stand, a bit more excited than usual, and Rosemarie decided to spend a few of her hard earned sou on a paper.

La Press de Picardie's headline screamed, "Assault on Ypres begins at Passchendaele." *If so, what is all the talk about Lille?* Rosemarie pulled Marcel to a bench.

"Maman, I want to go home," he fussed.

"Hush, hush, my love. Let me read." She caressed his hair, never taking her eyes from the paper. She read it from cover to cover, but found no mention of the Canadian Corps. She still had no idea if Harry was there.

Does it matter, Rosemarie? she wondered again and feared not. She devoured any mention of the Canadians, but the fighting raged north and east of Amiens in a jagged line that staggered northwest like a drunken seaman. *Why for God's sake did they open another assault? Shouldn't they wait for the American forces?* She didn't think Passchendaele, a Belgian crossroads could, matter that much.

"Maman? Bad news?"

She looked down to see concern in Marcel's little face. She wanted to howl at the heavens, but she couldn't. She forced herself to smile.

"No bad news, my love. Shall we read tonight after dinner?"

"D'YA THINK the Yanks will be deployed at Passchendaele?" Laporte said over a tin cup of weak tea. They sat in the shelter of a dripping tarp near Lens, while the sound of bombardment vied with thunder around them.

"Harvey says the word is they haven't done much but march through Paris. Pershing says they need training." The lieutenant was good for army gossip if not much else. His predilection for hanging out with British officers had that much benefit.

Laporte's string of creative cursing in two languages made his opinion of the need for training clear. "Give them to us. We'll train 'em up good," he concluded.

"There aren't that many of them here yet," Mac said.

"At the rate they're coming, we'll have the Huns wiped up before they put a boot on the front line," Laporte spat.

"We can let them scrub the floor after the party," Willard suggested, bringing a ribald list of what kind of housecleaning the foot-dragging Yanks could do from Trottier, Walker, and even Sullivan. The boy had a sharper edge to him since Vimy.

Harry kept his counsel. He hated to inflict this war on anyone, but he wished they'd speed it up if they were going to be any help. The chances of the war ending in 1917 grew dimmer by the day, and the men's elation over Vimy faded as the Battle of Arras ground to a stalemate, casualties mounted, and they fought back over territory a second and third time.

The current exercise in futility, the effort to take a hill that didn't even have a name—the army called it "70"—just so they could control the empty derelict town of Lens because some benighted planner thought it controlled the way to Lille—made him sick at heart. Harry didn't want Lille any more than he wanted to be sitting in a sodden tent with four muddy men listening to complaints, but here he sat.

When he closed his eyes, the mud in his lashes glued his lids shut. He let them stay, crawled inside himself, and tried to conjure up images of Rosemarie at *les hortillonnages*. The shock of her appearance in Arras had rattled his carefully cultivated fantasies, and they had turned more lascivious and darker every time he closed his eyes. He feared that when he finally saw her again, he might not want to recognize his own actions.

"Time to move out," Mac called.

"Again," Trottier muttered.

Harry rubbed a hand to clear his eyelashes and blinked his eyes open. He shoved thoughts of Arras aside and deliberately consigned Rosemarie and Marcel to the safest place he could build in his imagination, his grandmother's house in Saskatchewan, as he had begun to do daily. With her carefully protected, if only in his mind, he closed his mind's door on them and prepared to face the assault.

He rose to pin each man in his squad with a speaking glance. "Okay, you mudders. Let's show them what Canadians can do. Maybe this time Sergeant McNaughton's ladies will keep up."

CHAPTER 13

By November, the last of Rosemarie's produce had been sold, jarred, or stored in a root cellar, and the wind blowing in from the sea to the northwest grew sharper. At the end of the second week, she edged her *barque* further upstream toward British headquarters. The harried men who staffed the mail had grown accustomed to this weary French woman and her little son bringing her letters every week or two. Sometimes one paused in his labors long enough to slip Marcel a bit of chocolate when she wasn't looking, so he always went enthusiastically no matter how tired he was from his days in the care center of the workshop.

This time the clerk who took her letter turned back abruptly. "Rosemarie Legrand? Wait here. I think I saw something." He disappeared to the back and returned moments later with a letter.

"You get your mail from some priest at the cathedral?" She nodded. He glanced down at the missive in his hands, seemed to consider his choices, and shrugged. "Can't hurt to give it to you, you coming here faithful, like."

He handed her a piece of mail addressed in Harry's familiar scrawl. She gaped at it and felt its heft. This one had more than a few words, from the weight of it. She cradled it in her hand as if it were Harry himself, savoring the feel.

When a man pushed past her, she realized others waited, so she made her way out to the quay, lifted Marcel into the little boat, and tucked the letter in her blouse.

Time enough to read it at home.

Early dark fell by the time she pulled up to her dock, and the little cabin felt damp and cold. She put a few sticks of wood into the stove and lit a lamp. *I'll have to spend some of my pay on fuel this year,* she thought wearily. *Thank God we have it.* Soon she had sausages heating and bread and milk ready for her little one. The last of the fresh tomatoes completed their supper.

"Uh, uh—pray first Marcel!"

"Thank God for food and for Maman and take care of Harry," he prayed, as he did every night, before tucking into his meal. She wondered sometimes if he knew for whom he prayed, if he even remembered the tall Canadian who had so enriched their lives the year before, but then she would see him with his little hand-carved boat and think he did.

With supper finished, dishes tidied, and Marcel content at play, Rosemarie sat in her rocker and took out Harry's letter.

"We had a bit of fun today," it began, warming her heart and drawing out a smile. He went on to describe a birthday celebration for a man named Sullivan. "He claimed nineteen years, and he needs every one of them, since he enlisted a full year ago. We're all pretty certain he lied then to get in and lied now, but none of us tells him that. He's a kid, Rosemarie, as you would see in a moment if you met him. At least he was a year ago, before—" A splotch followed before, as if he started to write more and jammed the pen down. Instead he wrote, "You know. This."

The letter went on to describe jokes at the boy's expense and the gift of a razor because the one named Laporte told him "you finally need it." Harry had scratched out a few words she thought said "the men," and she pursed her lips ruefully. She could imagine where a band of soldiers might take a boy on the brink of manhood to induct him into grownup mysteries. Plenty of those sorts of places followed the troops. *Did Harry make use of women of the night?* She shook the thought away; it didn't bear consideration.

The rest of the letter lit a fire in her heart. "You can tell from this that things are quieter, slowing as they do with winter coming. I'm hoping I can talk the captain into leave, my lieutenant being useless. I can't promise, but with luck he'll let me go for a few days so I can come to *les hortillonnages* and you."

Her spirits soared. *Harry may come!* She looked around her, taking stock. This time she could prepare, fill the larder, and celebrate a bit.

"MAIL CALL, YOU SLACKERS," McNaughton called, and began handing out letters.

Sullivan colored at the ribbing he got over yet another letter from his mother, three this time, actually. Nothing for Laporte. Two for Willard.

"Two for you, Corporal," Trottier said, studying the remaining mail.

Harry stepped up and took both.

He ignored Mac's raised eyebrow. He put Rosemarie's in his shirt for later and glared at the other. The men drifted away to read their mail or mourn the lack of it.

"Still tossing your da's mail unread, Harry?" Mac asked. "Shouldn't you at least open it?"

"Don't need to. Mother would write if anything important happened."

"She writes whether something important happens or not," Mac observed. The sergeant clutched a letter of his own.

"Not today. This one's on his office stationary like every

month. I can recite it without looking. 'Look to your future, Henry. Apply for promotion. Spend time with the British officers, they'll have influence when this is over.'"

"Drives you mad, does he?"

"Always did. He still thinks I'm going to law school."

Mac chuckled. "Horrors, the man wants his son to succeed. What a bastard!"

"Sarcasm doesn't become you, McNaughton."

The sergeant shook his head. "You're still fighting another war, the one you left behind when you enlisted. You'll need to settle it one day."

"We'll settle it when he realizes I know my own mind."

"I swear, Harry, when the subject of your da' comes up, you sound as young as Sullivan."

The two men peered down the trench where Sullivan bent over a letter on pink paper, sadness stark in his eyes.

"I think that one isn't his mother," Mac said slyly. "Nor the one you dropped in yer shirt neither."

Harry put a hand over his heart where the letter rested. "Whatever my father says, this is my future."

He would savor her letter slowly, even though he already knew what that one held as well: the progress of her garden, Marcel's newest vocabulary, the cathedral on Sunday, the weather. There would be no pressure, no worries, no reports of violence. After Arras she understood he needed to envision her at *les hortillonnages*.

I love her for it, he thought. *I* love *her!* He knew it in the marrow of his bones. *But have you told her, Harry?* Of course he hadn't. *"I love you" would be as good as a promise. With death hanging over me every day, how can I?*

CHAPTER 14

Rosemarie rolled out dough for baking on December twenty-third, grateful she had a son to give her reason to go on each day. Of Harry she had heard nothing since the letter about Sullivan with its seductive promise of a visit.

No, not a promise. He merely dangled hope, hope that dwindles every day. The thought dampened her Christmas joy.

She covered the dough with sugar and pieces of fruit—sparse enough, but far more than she had the year before. Between what she could hold back from selling and what she could stretch from her pay, Christmas baking had become possible again. Marcel, making pictures on scraps of paper at her scarred kitchen table, hummed with contentment.

Be grateful for what you've been given, Rosemarie. Don't long for what you cannot have.

A sound so faint she almost missed it came from the door. She twisted her head in the window to see the canal in front of her island. A boat pushed way, poling toward the city.

"Someone at the door, Maman?" Marcel asked, looking up from his drawing.

She wiped her hands on her apron and pulled the old wooden door open. The caller, dirty and travel-worn, must have been leaning on it because he dropped forward when she opened it.

"Harry!" She sank to her knees in front of him, and he lay his head down on her shoulder.

"Sorry. I just— I couldn't—"

She put her arm around his shoulders and cupped the back of his head. "We haven't heard from you since you told us about Sullivan's birthday," she said with a smile she hoped would cheer him.

It had the opposite effect. His body began to shake. "Oh God, Sullivan!" She realized then that he wept, deep heart-rending sobs dragged from inside; he clung to her as a drowning man who would reach for any piece of flotsam that might save him, and cried.

She held him in the doorway for long minutes, but when the cold wind from the water threatened the fragile warmth of the little cottage, she pulled him forward into the kitchen. He went meekly, too wretched to object or even notice, clinging to her as she moved him.

"Marcel, the door," she directed, and the boy ran to shut it behind them.

"'arry?" he asked. "Is he sick?"

"Sick at heart I think, and very tired." She waited until the worst of the sobs subsided with Marcel leaning on her side staring wide-eyed at his idol.

She wondered when he had eaten last but suspected exhaustion—physical, emotional, and spiritual exhaustion—was the most pressing problem. "Harry, can you hear me? When did you sleep last?"

He made a movement that may have been a shrug. A moment later he choked out an answer with a note of bitter laughter in his voice. "Sleep? I don't recall."

"Come with me." She pulled him to his feet, and he staggered against her to the stairway. "We can talk when you've rested." She pushed him ahead of her on the narrow stairs.

"Rested, good," he mumbled, holding himself erect with one hand on each wall while he lurched from side to side up the narrow stairs.

They reached the low-ceilinged room, and he had to duck, leaning on her as she tried to maneuver his big frame. "Let's get you into my bed and then—"

"Your bed...yes." He fell backward onto it, pulling her down with him, and began to kiss her face, the tears on his cheeks leaving hers wet, but his actions quickly slowed, and his eyes drifted shut. When Rosemarie wiggled out of his arms, the sleeping man didn't stir. She stood, arms akimbo, taking inventory of dirt and damage. Bloodstains on his shirt had her ripping the garment open.

Not his. No visible wounds, thank the good Lord.

She removed his boots and swung his legs around onto the bed. Even when she removed his trousers, he didn't stir. The grimy shirt proved more problematic, and at one point he murmured her name as if to ask question, but he sank back onto the pillow, deep into sleep.

HARRY WOKE with a stab of fear. He reared up, groping for his rifle, afraid he had fallen asleep on duty.

He sank back into the bed as awareness flooded in. No enemy lurked. He reposed in soft covers in an unfamiliar room, his clothes had gone missing, and he wasn't alone. A small boy watched him steadily from the doorway. Memory flooded back— fleeing from Lens, frantic to get to Rosemarie. He hadn't deserted; he'd gotten leave or rather had it thrust on him with orders from Captain Mitchell to come back whole. He remembered a frantic journey, reaching her cottage, falling against the door, and not much else.

"You are dirty," the boy said, approaching the bed. Harry ran a hand across the stubble on his face. It came away filthy.

"Apparently so. And you are tall, much too tall to be Marcel."

The boy stiffened in offense. "I am Marcel. I am three." He held up three fingers.

Before Harry could think what to say next the boy ran to the stairs shouting, "Maman, 'arry is awake!"

His soldier's instinct took stock of his surroundings. The room spread out under peaked roof beams. He doubted he could stand upright anywhere but the center of the room; it had only one way out, the direction Marcel had taken. He had slept in an actual bed. *Rosemarie's bed, it has to be. Did we share it?* He thought not. *If we had, I would certainly remember.*

The blankets he lay in were worn and mended, but warm enough and clean—at least they had been until he lay in them. Since whoever took his clothing left his drawers and nothing else, he thought it best to stay nested where he lay. A tiny window at the peak of the roof let in a beam of light. It appeared to be slanted low in the sky. *Does that window face east or west? Did I awake at dawn or sleep round the clock?*

He could hear the boy talking with his mother and the sounds of pots and pans. Sharp awareness told him one more thing. *Somewhere in this haven, fresh bread baked, sweet dough*, he thought. His mouth began to water. With that, came the realization of gnawing hunger.

He debated what to do, undressed and feeble as he was. He envisioned Rosemarie fussing over her baking, and an even greater hunger overcame him, one he might do well to tame before he got out from the covers.

Her appearance in the doorway, his own vision of heaven itself, carrying a basin of steaming water, saved him the decision.

She put it on the little three-drawer chest against the opposite wall, along with the towel and rag she had over her arm.

"You'll want to wash up," she said. "I'm sorry we have no bathing tub. I found Raoul's robe in storage," she added, pointing to a purple robe draped over a trunk. The trunk, Marcel's pallet at the foot of the bed, and a chest of drawers furnished the tiny room. She looked oddly shy, as if having him tucked in her bed with her late husband's things nearby made her awkward.

Raoul. He had forgotten the husband, long dead now. The acid of pointless jealousy ate at him, and he could think of nothing to say. He sat up, letting the blanket fall to his lap, and her eyes dropped to the floor, but not before he caught the heat when she spied his naked chest. The jealousy fell away.

Harry swung his feet to the floor, pulling one of the covers across his lap with him, but deliberately giving her a view of his unclothed parts. "Thank you. I must look a mess," he said, rubbing his stubble. His voice sounded rough as if he had swallowed gravel.

"I forgot."

She scurried from the room, leaving him disappointed. *You damned fool. You think to tempt a woman in your dirt?* Harry sighed. He padded to the basin and leaned over it, enchanted by the warmth and the scent of lavender.

She came back momentarily with a small bundle tied with straps. "I found this as well. I meant to sell it last year, but never found a way." She handed it to Harry, who found a straight razor, plain and serviceable, inside.

"When you're ready, come down for your breakfast. Or supper, perhaps. You've slept the clock around."

Not dawn then.

He opened his mouth to thank her again, but no words came out. They studied each other—Harry trying to memorize every line of her face and hair, and Rosemarie scrutinizing him from his bare feet to his bare chest to the unruly hair on his head. He didn't know if she took stock searching for signs of damage, or simply lusted. Either way, it warmed him utterly. He turned toward the chest of drawers, sparing her blushes, and he heard her steps softly descending.

A warm kitchen, sweet rolls, and a woman's attention constituted Harry's idea of heaven until the need to touch the woman out of reach formed his personal purgatory. She had fussed over him until he ate his fill—an activity that took a while—and then poured herself coffee when she refilled his mug, and sat across the table.

Marcel had hovered nearby, alternately clinging to his mother's side and reaching toward Harry as if to confirm he was real. Harry reached for the lad, and the little one came into his lap eagerly. Wrapped in a robe sizes too small with a blanket around his legs, Harry cuddled Marcel against his shoulder, sipped his coffee, and waited for Rosemarie to speak. Harry had no idea what to say or where to start.

"You have leave." It wasn't a question.

"A whole week this time."

Her joy at that statement exploded across her expressive face. "You told me the war slows in winter."

His heart pinched, and his chin fell to his chest. *Not fast enough. Not thoroughly enough.*

She must have seen something in his face, because her hand reached across the table to touch his arm. "Tell me about Sullivan," she murmured.

The pinch became a violent cramp, and he grit his teeth against it.

CHAPTER 15

She would have taken back her words if she could have. Whatever had happened to Sullivan, Rosemarie believed he needed to tell her, but when he didn't respond, she wondered if he could. The pain in his face broke her heart.

"Dead," he choked out at last. He took a deep, shuddering breath and glanced down at Marcel, laying one of his large hands against the boy's head. "It happens in war," he murmured. His eyes seemed to plead with her.

It isn't fit for a child's ears. Of course. What was I thinking?

"Your uniform is almost dry," she said, indicating his clothing hanging on a wooden rack near the stove.

"Thank you. I feared I would wear a blanket forever," he replied with the ghost of a laugh, loosening his grip on Marcel.

"I couldn't get the stains out of your coat." His stricken look alarmed her. "Will you come to midnight Mass with us?" she asked, as much to distract him with a pleasanter topic as anything.

"Is my friend the *abbé* still at the cathedral?"

"Certainly."

"How could I not go see him?" he said. "When is it?"

"Tonight, you foolish man. It is Christmas eve."

His jaw dropped. He glanced at the window where light had faded.

"I told you that you slept around the clock," she told him. "You needed it."

"But Christmas already? I almost missed it. I tried…" He sighed deeply. "I have no gifts." His crestfallen look tore at her. *How can he worry about something so trivial after what it obviously cost him to even get to us?*

"Last year your gifts blessed this house. They saved us. This year, I can give, and you will receive. Isn't that how—" She almost said, "how love is," but caught herself. "How people get on. Sometimes we give. Sometimes we receive gifts. It is my turn to be the giver." She regarded him closely, silently begging him to let go of his pride and accept her words.

His smile, when it came, looked infinitely sad, but he nodded. "Thank you," he whispered. Marcel hopped down and went and fetched the little *barque* and boatman Harry had carved the previous year. He grinned up at the weary soldier as if to say, "See, I already have a gift."

Rosemarie watched Harry's eyes grow watery, and she rose to her feet, bustling about the coffeepot to save his male vanity. "More?" she asked, bringing a plate of sweet rolls. He devoured yet another one. "But eat quickly because we need to dress if we're going into Amiens."

～

LONG HOURS later they returned in the dark, a lantern lighting their way, Harry holding a sleeping Marcel in the bow, and Rosemarie poling the *barque* with confidence born of long familiarity. Candlelight and music had calmed Harry, and Rosemarie hoped they had given him some peace. It had been a respite from the war in any case.

They had lingered by the crèche outside the church, drawn by the carolers and good cheer. *Abbé* Desjardin greeted Harry like a long-lost brother and invited them in for a nip of wine. In the light of the priest's office, the dark shadows in Harry's face appeared less stark, but his exhaustion had been clear. He needed bed, and soon.

When they reached her dock and she tied up, she wondered if it wasn't already too late. Both Harry and Marcel slept in the stern cuddled together like puppies. Rosemarie had to tie the *barque* firmly before she could kneel on the dock and reach for the sleeping boy. She had no idea how she could get the man out of the boat if he didn't wake up.

"Harry," she called softly. "We're home." He didn't move. She tugged at Marcel, pulling him from the sleeping soldier's arms. "Harry, wake up," she repeated.

He stirred then. "Home?" he murmured, blinking his eyes open and pulling himself upright. In the harsh lantern light she couldn't miss the haunted sorrow buried deep behind his lids, the faint echo of yearning in his question.

"Yes. Home. My home—yours for tonight."

His eyes widened, and a sad smile came over his face. He stepped onto the island beside her. "Home," he repeated.

She led the way, every fiber in her being conscious of his presence and the heavy weight of his grief as he followed her inside. Whatever peace he found in the singing and the liturgy had dissipated when they crossed the river.

I should go. He couldn't make himself say it. *I should go.*

Stooping to enter Rosemarie's refuge along *les hortillonnages,* he took his darkness with him. He knew she deserved better. Marcel deserved better. *The boy is entitled to a happy Christmas joy, and his mother, hope.* Harry could provide neither. He stopped just inside the door, arms slack at his side.

She turned to gaze at him quizzically, but asked no questions. "I'll tuck him in. You rest." Before he could object, she disappeared above stairs leaving Harry to peer around the room searching for rest as if it could be found. He took in the tiny *arbre de noel,* more of an evergreen branch really, that she had placed in the window and decorated with bits of foil and red paper. The crèche, of course, had pride of place, set on more evergreens on an overturned box to raise it from the floor next to the iron stove.

Rosemarie stepped down the stairs holding his grandmother's Bible, and looked at him quizzically when she found him locked in place, still standing at the door.

"I—" he began, but he still couldn't say it. He struggled not to crumble when faced with the concern he saw on her face.

She set the book on the kitchen table without a word and took his hand to half lead, half drag him to the battered rocker at the far side of the room, near the little stove, where she pushed him down. Her hand came up to cup his cheek. "Would you like tea?"

He shook his head and slumped against the back of the chair, weariness like an iron chain holding him down.

"What can I get you, Harry?" When he didn't answer, she dropped to her knees next to him. "How can I help?"

He had no answer. Her head dropped to his knees, and for a long moment, he thought she would say nothing. He was wrong. She spoke without raising her head. "Tell me about Sullivan, Harry. You said his name when you stumbled through my door. I think that's why you came."

Sullivan. Oh God! His eyes burned; tears choked him. *Is that why I came?* He wanted to deny it. He could not.

"I'm sorry. My burdens aren't yours. You deserve better."

"Trust me with your story, Harry. Tell me what you need to tell me. Your letter said you celebrated his nineteenth birthday."

"He lied." He looked at her then; he saw her expression—open and generous, ready to take in whatever pain he shared. He swallowed and went on. "I doubt if he was much past sixteen. A boy. They make it sound glorious, the recruiters. What boy could resist?"

The shadow of sorrow enveloped her as he dreaded, but she faced him bravely. "What happened after you wrote?"

He wanted to stop his story, but once begun he couldn't. "Our rotation came up—one more attempt to dislodge the damned Germans." He spoke faster, trying to explain. "I always keep Sullivan with me, behind me if I can. We were halfway across when we came under fire. He was behind my right shoulder, where I wanted him." He leaned forward and patted his right shoulder with his left hand, showing her, needing her understanding. He twisted to his left. "I turned to the left to order the squad down." His eyes held hers, needing her to see what haunted him. "For a moment. It only took a moment. I turned—" He choked.

"What happened, Harry?"

"Sullivan came around on my right in front of me. I heard the shot. I heard—oh God, I heard it hit. The sound—" He gagged. "It should have been *me*. He walked in front of *me*."

She was in his lap then, though he didn't remember her moving. She held him while he swallowed back nausea, caressing his head and murmuring soothing sounds.

He had to finish; he went on, his words muffled in her hair. ""He fell back against me. I wrapped my arms around him and fell into a shell crater, the others with me. He looked at me as if he wanted to ask something. His—" *No. She doesn't need to know what happens to a man's face when a bullet rips through it.* "A moment only. The question disappeared, and there was nothing left. Nothing."

Shudders racked him; only the security of her arms kept him from flying to pieces. He buried his face against her neck.

A moment later—or perhaps an hour—he didn't know—she lifted his face with one gentle hand and kissed him tenderly. He meant to return it in kind but found gentleness impossible. Hunger for the solace she offered, the peace she represented, took over, and he plundered her mouth ruthlessly, turning her in his arms so he had better access.

Rosemarie clung to his neck, but he didn't know if she welcomed his assault or held on in desperation. One arm anchored her in place while his other roamed across her body, seeking and exploring.

This is Rosemarie, a distant voice reminded him. *She's meant to be cherished.* He tried to ignore it, but he could not. He stood abruptly, placing her on her feet. "I'm sorry, I—"

She silenced him with one hand. "Don't be." She stood on tiptoe and kissed him again. "You need rest. Let me put you to bed."

Bed. Lascivious thoughts raced ahead. "If you take me up there, sleep is the last thing I'll want. I should sleep by the fire as I did before."

She opened her lips as if to argue, and he took her mouth in his again. This time there was no mistaking her response, and he couldn't resist the surge of triumph it gave him. He pulled her back down into the chair, his mouth never leaving hers, one hand slipping inside her blouse to find her ripe breast erect and ready. He smiled against her mouth. "This chair may be a better chaperone than your bedroom but not by much."

She silenced him with her mouth, yet he pulled back, his eyes boring into hers. *She deserves respect*, the voice said. *She deserves marriage.* He argued with his conscience. *How can I marry her with death waiting for me?*

"I want you Rosemarie—"

She laughed at that bit of nonsense, her hand across his trousers reminding him how obvious that was. He pulled her hand a few inches away and went on before she could say anything. "But we are in no position to marry." *Fool. You haven't asked her, and you can't make promises. Not now. Not yet.*

She began to respond, but he rushed on. "Even if we were, the last thing you need is another baby. Worse. I— I can't promise I'll make it through the damned thing, and I won't have you alone again with another little one to feed." He gave her shoulder a shake. "Even if you want to take that risk, I won't have it! If I got you pregnant, I would be in terror every day. Do you understand? How could I do what I have to do worrying about you here more than I already do?

HE MEANS WHAT HE SAYS, and he's right of course. Even in grief he's wiser than I am. Still... "Pleasure me then, Harry. Let's give each other that much at least." She wanted to beg and hated herself for it. His big hand, warm on her breast squeezed and began to move, however, and her head fell back across his arm. His mouth came down to meet hers again.

When she lay shuddering in his arms some time later, disheveled and wet, it occurred to her the chair had been less of a chaperone than he intended. He cradled her head on his shoulder, his head against the back of the rocker, and she thought he dozed off. She kissed the bare skin between the open sides of his shirt and slipped one hand back inside the open fly to his trousers, when his hand clamped on her wrist to stop her. Their eyes held for a long moment before she gave in and lay back against him.

"I can't promise anything," he murmured. "It isn't over," he said. "I have to go back."

The darkness began to close in, but she refused to surrender to it. "How much longer can it be? The Americans are in it now." She wanted to believe the end was near. She had to believe it.

His head moved from side to side. "We haven't seen them in the field. I don't want you to have false hope."

She turned her face into his strong chest, not wanting to hear his despair.

"Will you write to me again?" she asked, her voice thick and muffled. *More often please. Every day.*

He didn't answer her. Instead he said, "When I'm out there, when we're about to go forward, I imagine you safe. I put you in my grandmother's kitchen—you and Marcel. I imagine you sitting at the table with her." His eyes searched hers. "Then I shut the door. I make myself believe you are there. Safe. It's the only way I can make myself move forward. Do you understand?"

She didn't. But she nodded. It was what he needed. She clung to him then in the night, holding on as long as he let her.

A long while later he spoke again. "I can't promise anything," he repeated, "but know that I will come back if I can. If I'm able."

If I survive. He didn't say it, but her heart heard it. She had no response. She lay in his arms staring into the darkness, until tiny sparks of light flickering above the treetops in the window caught her attention.

"Look," she said, pointing to the window. He followed her gesture.

"The sky has cleared," he said.

"There is no moon, and it is lit with a million stars. When I see them, I'll think of you. I'll know you see them too."

She felt as well as heard him clear his throat and swallow hard. "I don't know when, but at the end, when the war is over—if I possibly can—I'll come for you and Marcel."

He offered all he could, no words of love, no promises. She accepted what he gave and searched for words for what she felt, words that wouldn't burden him.

"I will wait. And Harry, I want to see your grandmother's kitchen."

He pulled her closer, and they dozed by the fire. Her last conscious thought contradicted his warning. *The war will end soon —it must. He will return.*

PART III

———

THE ELEVENTH HOUR

CHAPTER 16

Amiens, France
February 1918

Harry returned as Rosemarie hoped, a flying overnight visit in early February with haunted eyes, chocolate for Marcel, and little news. He once again refused her bed, alluded ominously to military preparations that made leave impossible, and held her with a desperate tenderness that left her heart restless even while he cherished her body. By morning he had disappeared, leaving a hole in her heart, raw and bleeding.

She toiled at the Amiens workshop daily, amazed that the city continued to function in the face of war, although awareness of the utter devastation just beyond the edge of their little world hung over its citizens like a pall, and memories of what she had seen at Arras haunted her nights.

Rosemarie grasped at hope when a letter came from Harry in February. He asked after Marcel, wished her well, and added, "Of my life, I have no words. I cannot write. I'm sorry." None came after that, forcing her to swallow worry and build a bulwark in her heart against despair. Yet she sent weekly letters full of gardens and weather, children and feast days—anything to give him a sliver of peace—and prayed he got them.

War talk filled the workshop, and Rosemarie listened avidly. Rumors hinted that the allies moved troops toward Belgium, though details were scarce. The French remained on the eastern flank; the Arras campaign had failed in spite of the heroism at Vimy, and the Germans remained entrenched along a line northeast of Amiens. For three years their presence hung over the city like a boulder on the edge of a cliff, poised to drop onto any unsuspecting people below and crushing everything in its path; now it teetered.

"The Allies have held them off so far, surely they can continue," moaned Marcellina, from her seat at the sewing machine next to Rosemarie's. She said it at least once a week.

Others insisted, "The Huns are bogged down. They are just too stubborn to surrender." Still more voiced similar thoughts, but one question dominated everyone's conversation. "Where are the Americans?" February passed into March with no word that the Yanks, though pouring into France, had actually entered the fighting.

The first week in March, dreary weather, anxious adults, and a cold had left Marcel irritable and in need of soothing, and Rosemarie delayed in the nursery to give him what he needed. She arrived at her seat somewhat late, to have Marcellina waiting to pounce.

"Did you hear?" Marcellina demanded, her eyes wide with fear.

Rosemarie's heart stuttered. *What now?*

Marcellina didn't wait for a response. "The Russians surrendered. They made treaty with Germany!"

Rosemarie relaxed momentarily, but her mind raced. "How can that impact us? Surely Russia won't send troops into France."

Her co-worker plunged on, irritated by Rosemarie's calm

reaction. "Pierre says it frees the Huns up, don't you see? All those divisions they have in Russia . . ."

Rosemarie didn't hear the rest, as the impact of the words hit her. Free from the eastern front, Germany could pour troops into France before the Americans got themselves organized. *They know it will be over once that happens. They'll rush it. They'll— Dear God preserve us. Preserve Amiens!*

Speculation engulfed Amiens for days after that, fed by rumors of troop movement, before it subsided under the weight of anticipation and tension, its people exhausted by their fears. On the twenty-first of March, the storm broke, and Rosemarie awoke to the distant rumble of artillery to the west. Marcel crawled into her bed. "Thunder, Maman," he murmured sleepily.

"Yes, darling. A storm is coming." She fed him porridge with dread lodged in her heart and hurried into the city early.

"The Germans moved on St. Quentin," Corporal Butler greeted her without preamble. "They're throwing everything they have at it."

St. Quentin lay northeast of Amiens. The last she heard most of the Canadian Expeditionary Force remained far west of there. *But the line of battle is long and the fighting . . .*She prayed for Harry, and for his friends.

News came in waves all week, messengers often contradicting one another: fighting at Bapaume, Rosières, Albert, ever closer to Amiens. The corporal insisted the German advance had stalled. "Don't they always?" But Marcellina's cousin who drove supply trucks swore they had advanced swiftly. Another woman insisted her neighbor witnessed the Germans retreating. Soon enough it became clear that the offensive was pushing west when word arrived that the Germans had crossed the Somme. From Harry, Rosemarie heard nothing.

Shelling remained at a distance, but the occasional shot came close, too close. She refused to alter her routine, if only for Marcel's sake, but she packed a satchel with a change of linen,

Marcel's little bear, and Harry's Bible. She kept it next to the door and prayed she wouldn't need to flee.

Lieutenant Harvey, you stupid, stupid man!

Harry watched the life ebb out of the man he had despised and tried to draw up some sympathy. He couldn't. At least the lieutenant didn't leave a wife and children. As near as Harry knew, he didn't leave a grieving mother either.

"Why in God's name did he crawl out of his cave now? He's gotten away with it for over a year," Harry said, staring down at the crumpled body.

"Brass must have threatened him. This mission wasn't much of an action. Dumb ass probably thought he'd be safe with us," Mac replied.

Their platoon had been sent to reconnoiter an empty hillside, one believed to be neutral, and occupy it if they could. Only it wasn't. The damned hill lay a good distance from the thick of the fighting, but a single German sniper, a boy not much older than Sullivan, had hidden there. They nailed him as soon as he fired, but it was too late for Harvey.

The kid had good aim. Harry would give him that.

"Want we should carry him back, Sergeant?" Laporte asked. They all knew how often the dead had to be left where they lay, how often they buried enemy dead to avoid contagion and left their own. No one said Sullivan's name.

Mac studied Harry. "My squad can hold here. Take yours and haul his worthless carcass back."

"Keep Trottier, Willard, and the rest," Harry replied. "Laporte and I will see him down."

The wiry Frenchman hefted the lieutenant's body, fireman-carry style, over his shoulders, and the two of them trudged back to the company headquarters where Laporte promptly dropped Harvey at Captain Mitchell's feet.

"What happened," Mitchell demanded. "That hill should have been clear. Did the damned fool fall on his rifle?"

"No sir," Harry said. "Huns had a sniper hiding up there. The shooter picked out his shiny clean helmet coming up, and drilled him. One shot."

"Did you get the bastard?"

"Willard picked him off before he could drop back down."

"Good." The captain drew a weary breath. "Haul Harvey back to the burial detail. I'll do the everlasting paperwork."

Harry and Laporte saluted and picked up their burden, this time Harry taking the load, and walked away, but the captain's voice stopped them.

"One more thing, Wheatly." Both men waited attentively. "You're in charge now."

Harry frowned. "Sergeant McNaughton—"

"You heard me, University Boy. You both did. You're in charge."

Harry cursed under his breath and ignored Laporte's sidewise glances, as they trudged past an ambulance that required six men to push it down the muddy, rutted road.

"They're going to make you a lieutenant," the private said eventually.

"Over my dead body," Harry answered. It probably would be. Lieutenants had the shortest lifespan on the battlefield.

CHAPTER 17

In early April, Rosemarie gave thanks when better weather improved her daily trip to Amiens by *barque*; that ended abruptly on the fourth when she arrived to the sound of shelling and the city in panic. She stepped off onto the quay to a scene of chaos, people loading their boats. Others unloading and putting household goods into hastily assembled wagons.

"What has happened?" she demanded of a wizened farmer she knew.

"They're coming!" he said, tossing bedding into a rickety cart.

"Who is coming?" she asked, dread growing.

"The Germans o'course. Pushing straight at Amiens and coming on fast." He hurried away.

Rosemarie took a deep breath, forcing calm.

"Maman?" Marcel asked.

"Let's go talk with *Abbé* Desjardin, poppet. He'll know what is real."

She found the priest packing.

"We've been ordered to evacuate, Rosemarie. It is time we all got out of the way of the fighting. I'm ordered to Paris." He shrugged sadly.

"But, *Abbé*, the soldiers say the German long range guns are hitting the capital! Surely we would be safer among the islands."

The old priest shook his head sadly. "Not if they are marching directly at us. You need to get Marcel out of the way of this thing, Rosemarie."

"I have no where to go, Abbé. My in-laws—"

He looked about to object, but they both knew Raoul's family had rejected her. "What about your Jacques cousins?"

"My cousin Remi's farm is above Rouen. We were close as children."

"Do you still hear from him?"

"Occasionally, but—"

"No 'but.' Gather your things and get Marcel away from Amiens," he told her, making shooing gestures.

"Harry thinks I'm at *les hortillonnages*. He'll—"

The old man stopped his packing and took both her hands. "Listen to me. Rouen has hospitals and depots for the British and their imperial troops. You'll be able to contact him from there. Go to Remi Jacques for help."

"I'll have to write to Remi and ask—"

"There is no time. You must evacuate and do it today."

Rosemarie wrote her cousin's name and the directions to his farm on a scrap of paper. "In case Harry comes looking," she said. The *abbé* took it and shooed her away.

She wandered back to the quay in a daze. *I should have brought my satchel with me.* Now she poled against the river traffic, back to *les hortillonnages*, with no idea what she might find.

CHAPTER 18

How can the stars still shine? Harry lay on his back on the cold ground, wrapped in a woolen army blanket, and stared at them. *But they do, and Rosemarie will see them.*

He clenched his teeth to stop their chattering. His squad—no, now it was his whole damned platoon—remained deployed near Ypres where they were kept busy in the business of killing and dying, but not busy enough. Harry longed to fight farther south where the big action had exploded. South. At Amiens.

He shook off panic, squeezed his eyes shut, and in his mind walked Rosemarie and Marcel up to the big farmhouse in Saskatchewan. Only when she was seated at the scarred old table, Marcel securely held in her lap, and a mug of cocoa in her hands did he feel safe. Only when she smiled over at his grandmother did he close the door and leave them there. He opened his eyes to the mud, the cold, and his stark loneliness. He looked up at the sky with its twinkling stars and thought of Rosemarie, clinging to her memory for a long moment.

"Mac? You awake?"

"Am now, your worship," his friend grunted. Harry knew he hadn't been sleeping.

"What do you think the colonel wants with me?"

"Going to make you official of course, Lieutenant."

Of course. It had been two weeks since Captain Mitchell told him he was in charge, and he just kept hoping they'd appoint someone else.

"Don't say that. Not yet. Should be you anyway. You're the soldier."

"Soldier yes, but I'm no officer. They'd never shovel the damned job on my plate, thank the good Lord."

"Damned snobs in Brit command. Two years of university and a father that's a lawyer and they think I'm officer material."

"Don't forget your Frenchie language skills and handsome visage."

Harry snorted into the darkness.

Mac rose up on one elbow; Harry could just make out his sober expression. "Listen to me, Harry. I've seen the way the men respect you. I know how things are done, but you know how to get them to do it."

"I hate what I have to make them do."

"Maybe, but better you than some yahoo they bring in like Harvey. Do it for my sake. You're a born leader. They'll follow you anywhere."

Harry stared back for a long while and then subsided, seeing only the sky. "That's what I'm afraid of," he murmured.

Just before he drifted off he heard Mac speak again. "I'll be with you every step, Harry. We just need to do the job and get them all home."

Home. Visions of Rosemarie lulled him to sleep.

The next morning he reported to division headquarters, saluted the colonel, and got formal orders. He didn't object.

Colonel Daniels, a baronet's son from Lancashire, appeared harassed and only mildly interested in his newest platoon leader.

"One question, Sir. What is the status of our Willard's commendation?" Harry thought he ought to make some use of the blasted promotion.

The colonel blinked at him. He obviously had no idea who Willard was.

"One of my men, Sir. He took out an entire gun placement singlehandedly at Vimy Ridge. Killed six and captured five others with their gun. Made them carry it down to headquarters. Lieutenant Harvey recommended for the Distinguished Conduct Medal." *After Mac and I bullied him into it.*

The colonel gestured vaguely at the major who served as his aide.

The man peered at Harry. "Willard? That the black soldier?"

"Yes sir. Remarkably good one," Harry replied.

"We have many good soldiers, Lieutenant," the major replied. The colonel sorted papers on his desk, already disinterested. Harry had been dismissed. They sent him off to get an officer's tunic.

Sorting through available supplies, Harry chose the shabbiest uniform they had, and he wondered fleetingly if Rosemarie had worked on any of the ones at the supply depot. They tried to give him a new helmet sure to gleam in the sun, and he wondered if they thought him a fool.

At least they no longer make lieutenants wear the gilded cuff badges that mark officers. Men had begun to refuse to wear them, so his new tunic had none. They gave him a pair of shoulder patches that were somewhat frayed, and he wondered what poor soul had worn them before he got them. He hoped it wasn't Harvey. He made mental note to dirty them up. It was one thing to be visible to his men and another to alert German snipers eager for target practice.

He reached his ride back to the trenches before a breathless corporal came running from divisional headquarters. At first Harry didn't react when the man called to him, as if "Lieutenant" must surely mean someone else.

The man slid to a stop and gave a smart salute. Harry

returned it, resigned that he'd have to get used to it. "What is it, Corporal?"

"Orders of the day, Sir. And also, this came for you." He handed Harry a folded paper and a thin yellow sheet, the telltale color of a telegram duly sealed with a sign it had been inspected. The orders could wait until he got back. He opened the telegram first, fearing bad news from home.

HEARD THROUGH CONNECTIONS. Thrilled with news. Well done, Lieutenant Henry Wheatly.

Father

HARRY CURSED UNDER HIS BREATH. *How the hell did he find out so quickly?* He shuddered to think about the man's "connections." He crumpled the telegram and tossed it away.

ROSEMARIE AND MARCEL arrived at her cousin's door hungry, bedraggled, and tired to be greeted by the deep frown from Elsa, her cousin's wife. Rosemarie had met the woman at Remi's wedding, but only a few times since, and had found her to be genial and friendly in the past. War and worry impacted everyone —often negatively—as it clearly had impacted this woman.

"I'm sorry, Elsa. We have no place else to go."

A boy a year or so older than Marcel peered around the woman's skirts, eying Rosemarie and her son.

"I'm hungry, Maman," Marcel said, eying the boy back. "You said we'd find food."

Rosemarie looked at the woman apologetically and was relieved that Elsa's expression softened when she glanced down at the boys.

"Come," she said at last. "I have soup and bread."

Remi came in from the fields to greet her joyfully, though his face fell when he realized she asked to stay, begging refuge and offering to work on the farm.

"Raoul's family cut us off," she explained. He knew she had no other family, and patted her hand sympathetically. She told him the sad story of her sister-in-law's accusations, the abbé's support, and her gradual winning back the support of neighbors. She didn't tell them about Harry, for fear they would think he sent her money. He didn't. She explained her job at the uniform workshop that was "closed now" and put her meager bag of savings on the table, earning Remi's gratitude. Elsa seemed to view it as the least she could contribute.

Her cousin's much warmer welcome came with burdens as well. Remi sipped weak tea and explained their struggles. "Don't mistake me, Rosemarie. We can stretch our resources to care for two more, but your offer of work matters. We have to grow and store as much as we can before winter. Those months will be dark and long. We must be disciplined now to survive then." He explained his tension between selling their produce at inflated war prices and conserving them. "What we grow is all that keeps us."

She nodded. "I understand. I can help Elsa."

The other woman spoke up. "I don't need help. I can cook and clean—even for two more if I must. Remi needs help in the fields."

Rosemarie managed a weary smile. If field work made them welcome, she'd embrace it. "I'm not afraid to get my hands dirty. I had to leave my little garden before it produced much." She thought of the spring greens left behind in the ground in her hurry and regretted not stopping for them.

Days passed before she finally told them about Harry. She debated whether to write to him that they had left *les hortillon-nages* because she knew he imagined them safe there, and it comforted him, but she believed he surely must know the Germans threatened Amiens. Besides, if he came for them as he promised, he needed to come to the farm. Driven by the need to let Harry know where they had gone, she finally opened up to Remi and Elsa after dinner one night.

"A Canadian, Rosemarie?" Remi asked, grinning at her.

"A good man, Remi."

"An improvement after Raoul," he said. He waved off her startled look. "I never thought he was good enough for you. I'm not surprised his family are such fools."

Elsa gave her a sharp look with no small amount of skepticism in it. "Can he not send you money?"

Rosemarie met her eyes directly. "What would I be if I took money from a man not my husband?" She held the woman's gaze until Elsa was forced to drop her eyes. "His assistance saved our lives last year," Rosemarie reluctantly admitted. She described Harry's gifts. "I need to write to him and tell him where I am. He will worry."

"Of course, you must," Remi agreed. "I can take your letter to the grocer who serves our post."

"It would better if I take it directly to the British army mail. I understand they are at Rouen and—"

Remi shook his head. "I can't spare the time away from the planting, nor the horse that pulls my plow to take you. Henri the grocer handles the post for us. He will take care of it." He shut the door on the matter firmly, and Rosemarie had to agree. She handed him the letter addressed to Corporal Harry Wheatly, in care of the army post, glad she had held back a few sou for postage when she handed them her savings.

She sighed deeply. "He will come for me when this ends. If he possibly can."

Her cousin and his wife stared back at her. Remi leaned over. "It won't be long then. The war can't last much longer."

Weeks turned to months, and the year dragged on. Even

when word came of the American victories at Cantigny and Belleau Wood, bringing their energy into the long stalemate, the denizens of the Jacques farm saw no sign the war would end quickly. Harry didn't reply to Rosemarie's letter or the one after that. The cost of postage prevented her from writing often, and the lack of replies left her empty of the will to write them.

This will end soon, she told herself nightly. *It must.*

CHAPTER 19

Harry let hope seep in when high command pulled the bulk of the corps back into Picardy after the German advances petered out in mid-July. The brass also implied they expected to make a stand between Amiens and the German army. He hadn't heard from Rosemarie since the German spring offensive, and his worries had given birth to more worries with every week that passed. Deployed just east of Amiens at last, Harry made one unauthorized dash for *les hortillonnages* with Mac covering for him.

The region close to the city appeared devoid of people; he couldn't blame residents from fleeing even as he filched a *barque* from under rushes up the Somme by some hopeful farmer who planned to return. He poled his way into the floating islands. The occasional stray shot from the big German guns had left its mark, but on the whole, the little garden spot appeared untouched. He came around the bend and saw Rosemarie's blue cottage and breathed a sigh of relief. He tied the boat and ran up the path.

The door opened at his touch, but the house lay silent before him. He didn't have to search; Rosemarie and Marcel were not there. Disappointment pushed him into the rocking chair. He squeezed his eyes shut and willed Rosemarie there, but when he opened his eyes, the house remained vacant, and Harry felt foolish. For one insane moment he considered waiting for them to return, but he could see they'd been gone for weeks, probably since the Germans moved on the city, and for that he should be grateful. Besides, he couldn't leave Mac for long, and only God knew when they would return.

God—and perhaps Abbé *Desjardin!*

He scribbled a note for Rosemarie telling her he had come and made it to Amiens without incident to find it only moderately damaged but eerily devoid of civilians and the cathedral offices in the care an elderly gent. The priests, he was told, had gone to Paris.

"Don't worry, sir," the old man said. "Those of us who didn't run like cowards protect the old church. Huns didn't get much of her."

"Most of the city evacuated." It wasn't a question.

"But many have returned bits by bits," the old man said. "We stand watch."

"Do you know Rosemarie Legrand?"

The old man screwed up his face in thought, adding yet more wrinkles to the puzzle that was his visage.

Harry assumed his answer would be no. "She is a friend of *Abbé* Desjardin," he prodded.

The old man's face lit up. "Ah. Raoul Legrand's widow? I know his sister Sabine."

"Do you know where Rosemarie went?"

"Sabine went to Marseilles."

"But Rosemarie."

The old man shrugged. "They don't get along." He made a sour face.

Understatement, that. Heaven only knows what the old witch said about her. Harry knew as little as he did before.

He thought about asking the man where he might write to *Abbé* Desjardin, but considered it fruitless.

He dragged himself back to his men, worries assailing him thicker than ever. *It should be a relief that she ran from danger, but did she make it safely? And where are they?*

When he reached the hovel they called his quarters, he found Mac pacing.

"About time you came, and good thing too. Moving in the morning, Harry." He indicated papers on the desk, obviously opened and read.

Harry glanced at the orders that looked little different than the previous dozen or more. "Briefing at dawn tomorrow," he muttered.

Mac leaned both fists on the table. "This is it Harry. This time is it."

Harry wanted to argue the point, but he knew what Mac meant. The allies—reinforced by the fresh troops from America—on one side, and the Germans—worn out—on the other. Worn out but desperate. "Maybe the beginning of an end. They won't go down easy."

"No," Mac agreed. "It will be bloody, and that's a fact."

Henri the grocer peddled up to Remi's door three months later, breathless and agitated. The nip of autumn air and suppressed excitement gave his cheeks a rosy glow. Rosemarie ran from the fields at the sight of him, expecting news, fearing it would be bad, and hoping he had a letter from Harry. The news stunned her.

"The eleventh hour of the eleventh day of the eleventh month," Henri exclaimed over and over. "They signed it this morning, and the guns stopped at eleven."

Over. Finally over.

Rosemarie groped for a chair and sat while Remi asked questions Henri couldn't answer. They didn't know the terms, but they knew Germany had surrendered just as they knew the kaiser had abdicated two days before.

"God help Germany," Elsa exclaimed. Her outburst was greeted by stares, but Rosemarie suspected she was correct. The allies would not be kind. Not after the hell of the previous four years. She understood but couldn't bring herself to care.

Where is Harry? Will he come for us now?

As if he read her mind, Henri walked over and took her hand. "Still no letter, *cheri*, but surely one will come soon, now that it is over."

His words jolted Remi from his elation. "Yes, Rosemarie. Even better, he will come for you soon, no?"

"Perhaps he will," Elsa added. "We can hope."

Rosemarie looked up into the woman's eyes, still blinkered with skepticism, and caught both sympathy and hope.

"He always comes for Christmas. You will be desperate for us to be gone before Christmas," she said.

Elsa opened her mouth and closed it. She tried again. "I won't lie. It would be a blessing to have fewer worries, but what will be, will be."

Remi dug around the root cellar and came up with a bottle of wine, carefully preserved for the occasion. He poured them all a glass and raised his in toast.

"To victory," he said. "To peace."

"To Rosemarie's Canadian. May he come for her soon," Henri added.

"To Christmas," Elsa added, "and joy for all of us."

Rosemarie's face burned. These people only wished her well. She hoped she could repay their kindness.

CHAPTER 20

December 22, 1918

> My dearest Rosemarie
>
> I can only hope my letters are reaching you, since yours seem to have gone astray...

Harry refused to believe Rosemarie had given up on him after she left Amiens. Even worse would be to believe she had been killed in the confusion.

No. That didn't happen. He looked back down and began to write.

> I haven't written since the armistice, hoping to tell you I was free to come to you, but we are still in camp in Belgium, waiting to hear whether we'll be the ones sent to occupy the Rhineland, or be free to go home. All I hear from the men is "repatriation." They've done the job and want to go home. Christmas approaches in a few days and still no word. It will be the first Christmas in three that I haven't been with you. Know that I'll come as soon as I can.

He twisted the pen in his hands and looked around. As

desperately as he wanted to beg leave and go find Rosemarie and Marcel, his duty lay in Ypres. "Camp" was a lie. Flying shrapnel had cut into his shoulder and landed him in the hospital. He should have been released before Christmas, or so the medics told him, but Laporte had come down with the Spanish flu, and he stayed to keep an eye on him. Some of Mac's squad had it too.

The rest of the platoon, kept away to avoid contagion, wanted daily updates on their hospitalized buddies. The men needed him, so he sat in a field clinic outside of Ypres worrying over men who had been through hell and expected him to look after them.

He couldn't leave; he could only write. The pen twisted back and forth while he tried to decide how to end it. There didn't seem to be more to say. Except *I love you desperately*. Or *You are my heart. I can't wait to marry you*. He'd never said any of those words to her, and it didn't seem appropriate to put them in a letter that could go astray. *What then? I miss you? See you soon?* None of those sounded right.

"Another letter, Harry? Maybe I'll get a job as a postman after this," Mac said, bursting in with a crate over his shoulder.

Harry scrawled his name and only that on the bottom of the note and folded it quickly.

"Where you going to send that one?" Mac asked.

Harry thought for a moment. "I'm going to try the cathedral again," he answered, scribbling down the address. *Not that it worked last time*. He added his direction per regulations of the military post, "Lieutenant Henry William Wheatly," with his unit information.

Harry glanced up at Mac. "What's with the box?" he asked, eying a crate that looked the worse for travel. Too big to be his grandmother's cookies, it didn't appear official either.

"Came for you this morning. Merry Christmas."

Harry eyed it warily.

"Well don't make me stand here guessing. Open the damned thing." Mac reached over and helped him pry the lid off. A letter on some sort of official stationary lay on top of something wrapped in tissue paper.

Harry picked it up and scanned the new letterhead. He waved it at Mac. "I should have read one of those letters."

Mac gave a low whistle. "Bloody Attorney General for the province? You really should read the man's letters. What does this one say?"

"*Deputy* Attorney General," Harry murmured while he read the letter through twice, both irritated and puzzled. "He says, 'You probably haven't had much use for this yet, but you will when you get home.'" His eyes met Mac's over the top of the box.

"Well," the sergeant growled, "take a look."

He lifted the tissue. "Damn it to the furthest bottom of hell. What is that fool thinking?" A ceremonial sword lay over the top of a lieutenant's dress uniform.

"Gol," Mac exclaimed. "Must've had that 'un custom made." The uniform came just this side of imposing on full ceremonial garb restricted to senior officers, but with lieutenant's badges. "Must plan on you parading around Regina—or maybe Ottawa—strutting yer heroic war record."

Harry just stared at it. Even for his father it was too much. "Burn it," he said at last.

"What? And waste all that? Man means well, Harry."

"No he doesn't. He wants to bask in some mythical reflected glory. He probably thinks it will help his career. Burn it."

"But when you get back to Canada—"

"Who says I'm going back there. I'm not going anywhere without Rosemarie. Maybe I'll just stay in France. Burn it, Mac."

Mac closed up the box and hefted it onto his shoulder, shaking his head. "Sometimes you show no sense at all," he said. He turned at the door. "The men are preparing to celebrate Christmas. You best be there to keep them from burning down camp."

Harry laughed. "Let them. They've earned it."

"They're threatening to break Laporte out of the hospital."

Harry's heart sank. "Best warn them, Mac. Laporte is failing. I'll sit with him. You get drunk for me. Willard will keep it from going too far."

Mac didn't argue; he turned to go.

"Burn it, Mac. That's an order."

"Maybe I'll use it. It will get me into one of the better brothels. How will your da like that?"

Harry's laugh, harsh and brittle, chased him out the door.

PART IV

THE LAST POST

CHAPTER 21

Kinmel Repatriation Camp, Wales
March 1919

"Damn it, I have my *Permission to Marry* form. How can I produce a marriage certificate if you won't give me leave to get married?" *How can I marry her, if I can't find her?* Harry felt sick at the thought—almost feverish. It had been over a year since he saw Rosemarie and months since he last had word from her.

"Permission ain't the same as married. Can't reserve a berth on th' repatriation ships without papers," the clerk repeated. "Plenty have 'em, and they come first. Most of t'other women are British. There are plenty here as willing as the Frenchies. Easier to find too." A sly look accompanied the infuriating suggestion.

He couldn't help Rosemarie and Marcel from a cell, and that's where he'd land if he pounded this officious little clerk into the ground. Harry's hands hurt from fisting.

"Let me speak to Colonel Daniels."

"Sorry, Lieutenant. Told you. Colonel's down with the flu. Camp's full of it." The worm's glittering eyes and sneering tone made his disrespect for officers plain. Since the armistice, discipline among the Canadian, largely working-class troops had eroded to open insubordination. Tension lay thick in the air, and no amount of sports or educational opportunities made up for the delays. Harry didn't blame them. They didn't fight their way through hell to rot in some Welsh training camp because the government couldn't get them home. The Americans were managing it efficiently enough.

His lieutenant's badges meant nothing to this clerk. Harry wished he had never taken the battlefield commission, but someone had to do the damned job, and he knew he did it better than the fools who were leading them. Now it hung around his neck like an anchor.

The clerk smirked at him, waiting for his next question, but what could he ask? He'd offer money, but with his luck the man couldn't be bribed, and Harry would end up in jail.

"Why'nt you send for her? Has she changed her mind?"

"No! I— It's just confusion. I need to go fetch her. To do that I need leave." In the waning months of the war, he hadn't worried about the lack of messages; more vital things than mail got lost in the cloud of war. Now, however, his fear grew daily.

He had written every week since his unit had been ordered into quarters in Wales. All letters addressed to her in care of *Abbé* Desjardin at the cathedral parish had been returned unopened with a note that she could not be found. When the *abbé* didn't respond himself, he addressed one to "the canons of Amiens cathedral," with no luck. Letters sent directly to the cottage received no reply. Harry swallowed rising bile when he thought of the sorts of things that could have happened.

The clerk shook his head. "Can't authorize leave, and the colonel is down for now. You'll have to wait. Ain't that what we're all doing?" It had been the same answer all week.

Harry stormed out of the office. Mac leapt up from his seat on the steps. "No luck?" he asked.

Harry didn't answer as he moved with long, loping strides toward the tiny room that served as a lieutenant's quarters. The only advantage rank gave him at this stage was a modicum of privacy.

Mac hurried after him. "I warned you," he said.

A growl deep in Harry's throat didn't deter the man. Not much Harry said or did deterred Sergeant Angus McNaughton. He had happily, if not always respectfully, celebrated Harry's battlefield commission, given, they both knew, as much for class and a university education as for actual performance on the battlefield. He'd become Harry's batman—but never his servant —he was Harry's friend.

Mac followed him into quarters. "Well?" he demanded.

Harry shook his head. "No leave. Daniels is 'unavailable.' "

The batman dropped his voice to a whisper. The walls in the hastily built officer's barracks were paper thin. "So what are we going to do?"

Harry sank onto his narrow bunk and leaned against the wall. Mac eyed him closely. "Are you okay? You don't look right."

Harry raised a shaking hand to run it through his hair. "No! I'm fine. I— I need to talk to General Fitzgibbon."

Mac whistled. "Go over Daniels's head? Better get that fancy dress uniform out for that one." He cast a gimlet eye on Harry's rumpled khakis, dropped to one knee, and waved a hand to tell the lieutenant to move his lazy feet so he could reach under the bunk.

"Told you you'd need it. Will take us a day to get the blasted creases out," Mac complained, his voice muffled under the mattress. He came out coughing, in a cloud of dust, pulling the packing case.

"And I told you to burn that thing," Harry muttered.

Mac opened the box and removed the object on top, the ornate ceremonial sword wrapped in soft wool. "Ought to wear this thing too. Can always skewer the general if he refuses to give you leave," he said.

When Harry made no objection to the outrageous threat, Mac looked up sharply and peered at Harry for a long moment before scrambling to his feet, cursing. "I knew you didn't look right." He flung his hand to Harry's brow and cursed again.

"Fever, Harry. And there's no 'almost' about it."

The Spanish flu had taken another victim.

CHAPTER 22

I should leave. I should go back to Amiens. Rosemarie dug for potatoes and tried to calm her raging doubts.

Two things kept Rosemarie at Remi and Elsa Jacques's farm. For one, there was no food on her tiny plot at *les hortillonnages* and no means to grow it for several weeks. The other—the big reason—was that the letters she had sent to Harry told him to look for them at Remi's. She had received no replies and had no way to know where he might look for them. Almost five months had passed since the armistice, however, and no word had come. She tried to believe he had been delayed by his duties. Alone in her pallet in the attic at night she feared he had forgotten his French lover and her son.

The previous month she had written to the British authorities enquiring about his whereabouts and giving her location. Their response left her terrified. "We have no record of a Corporal Harry Wheatly." Until then she hadn't allowed herself to believe he might be dead, one of the many mowed down during the final march into Belgium in October. First fear of desertion, now fear for his life plagued her.

Another shovelful yielded even more root vegetables. The diet might be tiresome, but no one was hungry in Remi's house.

Rosemarie worked steadily for several moments more before trudging back toward the farmhouse.

A man on horseback came up their lane—Remi had returned from town. Her foolish heart gave a leap of hope. Perhaps there was mail. The door to the house opened, and Marcel ran out to be greeted by their cousin with a pat on the head. Remi handed the reins over to the boy who loved the great beast that served the family. His willingness, though still short of five years old, to muck out stalls and care for it had done much to win Elsa's approval. Her own son had been more than happy to turn over the hated duties.

Rosemarie examined her cousin, ready with her question, but the naked sympathy in his warm brown eyes answered it for her. No mail for her again this week.

IMAGES AND SOUND—MAC'S craggy voice prominent among them —sifted in and out of Harry's feverish cloud. One moment Rosemarie snuggled next to him. The next he chased her through the nightmarish landscape that was the Valley of the Somme in the aftermath of Courcelette, all ruined houses, mud, and barren trees.

"Best come around. You're not going to like this one." Mac again. Harry suspected he didn't like much, but he couldn't remember.

"Doc says yer better, but you look like hell." Mac again.

Dour old sod. Harry screwed up his mouth in a mockery of a smile, but it hurt so bad he stopped. Light filtered through his eyelids. *Should I open them? It's morning.* With great effort he lifted eyelids that felt as heavy as hundred-pound howitzer shells to see the craggy face of his friend peering back.

"Well. There y' are," Mac said. He followed his words with a cool damp cloth, wiping Harry's face and moistening his cracked lips. "Welcome back. Y've been gone three days, and you'll be wanting to hear the news—though God knows you won't like it."

News? Harry struggled for a moment to remember where he was. *Belgium. No. The war ended.* "Rosemarie?" he rasped. When Mac didn't answer immediately, he squinted at the man's pained expression. *Bad news then.* Moisture pooled in his eyes.

"Not that, lad. Mostly no news on that front. The man you wrote to in Amiens says she hasn't been seen since the Huns moved on the city in April. Th' British brass—" Mac spat. "Those fancy boys respectfully informed you that tracking refugees on behalf of colonial officers ain't their job. Not bad news, Lieutenant. Just no news at all."

Then what is the old fool trying to tell me? Harry tried to ask, but his throat seemed disinclined to cooperate. He only managed to croak out one word, "What?"

"You've a problem coming right quick. Irritating the general's little brown socks off, too."

Harry blinked. *Get on with it.*

"The bloody Deputy Attorney General for Saskatchewan arrives from Liverpool in two days. Says it's some kind of 'fact-finding delegation.' General sent his aide-doo-camp in here this morning to see if you were in shape to be found."

Harry frowned. *Why the hell should I care about the Deputy goddamn Attorney— Wait.*

"Remembering are you?" Mac asked.

It tickled his consciousness and rose to the surface. "Hell!"

"You got that out clear's a bell," Mac chuckled.

He had stuffed the news of his father's appointment to the back of his mind. *Did he write that he was coming? Probably. Damn and double damn.*

The old man got all puffed up; that much Harry knew. He'd never stopped badgering him about returning to university so he could go on to law school. Never listened to what Harry wanted. Started in on hints of the government jobs he could get for his son, the stellar career a war vet might have if he played it right. The thought made Harry sick, so he just quit reading the letters. He was paying for it now.

"Yes, your doting papa in all his provincial glory will be here in two days. The general is not happy. He's ready to put you on the next ship out, one of the American ones if he has to."

"No!"

Mac sat and picked up a bowl. The smell of chicken broth turned Harry's stomach. "Easy for you to say." He spooned some into Harry's mouth and unleashed an explosion of sputtering and gagging.

"Rosemarie," Harry choked out.

"If you plan to stop the man from trussing you up like an infant and carrying you home in his loving arms, you best get well." Mac held another spoonful above his mouth.

Harry glared at the spoon, but the words sunk in.

Father is on his way to humiliate me. I need my voice back so I can tell him to go straight to hell.

CHAPTER 23

A tiny window let sunlight into the attic room Rosemarie shared with her son. The one place in the crowded farmhouse she could find privacy—at least when Marcel busied himself in the barn or chased about the fields with his cousins. Rosemarie sought it out when she had a moment free from work. She pulled out the battered English Bible that had brought Harry into her life when she retrieved it from the Somme, wet and muddy.

Her English had improved, but the scriptures still outran her skills. She let the sun through the tiny triangle of glass fall on her lap to warm her and simply held onto the book.

Please, God, bring my Harry to me. Please, God, let him be alive. Even news of him, God, I beg you.

Heavy tread on the narrow stairs interrupted her, and Remi poked his head up into the room, a wide grin on his face. "Something for you! Henri brought it out. He said it looks important and you wouldn't want to wait until I go into town."

Rosemarie put the book aside and rushed over. Remi began descending. "Come quick. He'll give it only to you."

Henri, the elderly grocer who served as their postman sat at stiff attention at Elsa's rough wooden table holding an envelope with both hands in front of him. When she stepped into the room, his brows rose, and he pronounced, "You have mail, Madame Legrand."

Rosemarie took the envelope with shaking hands and peered around at Elsa, Remi, and Henri, all watching her avidly. She squeezed her eyes shut for a moment, offering a swift prayer she would see Harry's familiar scrawl on the envelope.

She did not. Her shoulders fell at the sight of the official-looking message. Remi rushed to nudge her into a chair for fear she might fall.

"It's from the British army headquarters," she said. *Please let it be good news.*

No one answered, but all three watched and waited while she opened it. The news made her gasp, put one hand to her mouth, and crush the paper in the other. "He's alive," she exclaimed, swallowing hard. Relief from the burden of long-suppressed fear left her weak and shaken.

"What does it say? Where is your corporal?" Elsa demanded when the wait become unendurable.

"He isn't a corporal," Rosemarie said, her laugh shaken by her trembling. "He is a lieutenant. Lieutenant Henry Wheatly. That's why they didn't find his record before. I asked about Corporal Harry Wheatly. Someone double-checked, God bless the man."

"Good, I think. But is he in France?" Remi asked.

"Wales. It says, 'The Canadian Expeditionary Force is stationed in"—she stumbled over the name of the town—"Bodel-wyddan. The Kinmel Training Camp, they say." The rest of the message began to sink in. "Oh, Remi. They are there to be repatri-ated to Canada."

"Why hasn't he written to you?" Elsa demanded.

"The mails are just becoming more reliable," Henri suggested with a note of defensiveness. "Did you give him your address?"

"Yes. At least I sent it when we fled Amiens last summer, and twice more, but the war raged around the city then. I have no idea whether he got my letters or not."

"Then he may not know where you are, Rosemarie," Remi said gently. "You must go to him."

Pain shot through Rosemarie's heart, and hope faltered. "What if he's forgotten us? With the war over he must think only of his home. I don't think I can bear it if he—"

"You don't know that he's forgotten you, Rosemarie," Elsa said. "Now that you have his whereabouts, you must try. Write at least." The genuine sympathy in her eyes warmed Rosemarie and gave her hope. "Or perhaps Remi is right. Just go to him. Then you'll know. If he is the man you've described, he'll welcome you."

The following morning, Rosemarie, bundled against the winds of early March, bid farewell to Marcel. He clung to her knees while she tried to reassure him she would return home soon.

"But Harry didn't," he retorted, peering up at her with moist eyes.

"That's it, Marcel. I'm going to fetch Harry. Maybe he can come with me when I come back for you." She prayed it was so. She glanced helplessly at her cousin's wife.

Elsa handed her a bundle of bread and cheese for the journey as she pulled Marcel away, giving him a reassuring hug. Her cousin's wife couldn't entirely hide her hope that she would be relieved of two mouths to feed, but she said goodbye with warmth and affection, holding Marcel in an embrace. "Send word, Rosemarie. We will worry," she said.

Remi accompanied her to the coast, the two riding together on the great horse. Her cousin, companion of her childhood, provided solid, mostly silent, reassurance behind her.

Remi arranged room for them to sleep in the kitchen of an inn in Esquelbecq, a small village north of Calais, increasing

Rosemarie's sense of indebtedness. "I can never repay you!" she told him.

He shrugged. "Your Canadian soldier can repay me once you find him," he replied in tones that made it clear he had no worries. Rosemarie knew his family's fragile circumstances; the meager savings she gave her cousin almost a year earlier was long gone. She worried enough for both of them.

"What if I don't find him? What if he doesn't want us when I do?" She fretted.

Remi kissed her forehead. "You are strong and resourceful, Rosemarie. You will manage. As Elsa said, write to us. Marcel will be waiting."

The next morning, he found a sympathetic fisherman who agreed to take her across what the English called their "channel" for a few coins and helped her into the boat.

The fisherman pushed away and oared from the dock until the wind took the sails with a snap, and the little sailboat moved off toward the open water. Rosemarie waved farewell to her cousin one last time. Fear about what she might find in Wales tore at her, but she held to courage and turned, the wind blowing her hair around her head, to face her uncertain future.

Days later, Rosemarie stood, bedraggled and travel-weary, in front of a massive iron gate set between two stone pillars, each topped with the everlasting lion of England. She had endured *mal de mer*, insults, hunger, cold wind, sore feet, an omnibus open to the weather, and miles of walking. Only the thought of Harry kept her moving forward—kept her from running back to Marcel and the warmth of Remi's kitchen. Now she faced yet another obstacle, this gate that blocked the entrance to the Kinmel Camp. Worse, two armed guards glared at her and demanded to know why she thought she could enter.

"I'd have a go at you myself if they let you in, but they won't," one said. He examined her from toes to hair insolently before adding, "Even if you aren't much to look at. No females. Sod off."

Rosemarie clenched her teeth to hold back the scold the worm deserved for his insinuations. She needed to get to Harry and couldn't risk anymore opposition.

The other guard darted an angry look at his fellow and said more kindly, "Sorry miss. Wives only, and them with permission. Those are orders."

"But I am his wife," Rosemarie lied. She hadn't come this far to be turned away.

"French wife? Got proof?" the insolent guard scoffed.

Her heart sank. "I don't carry it with me."

"I'll just bet you don't."

"Sorry, miss," the other began again. "Ladies have no place in a military camp."

"The brass thinks we've had too many women trying to get transport, looking for a willing man to marry—or whatever." The other guard snorted, drawing a fierce glare from his partner.

People at the inn where she'd worked for her food the night before told her there was sickness in the camp. *What if Harry has the Spanish flu? So many young men have died.* "Please," she begged. "I heard he is sick. I can nurse."

The kinder guard squirmed uneasily. The other shouted, "Get you gone. We aren't here to chat with every tart who thinks she can come in and turn a few coins."

Rosemarie's cheeks burned. She shook her head in denial and opened her mouth to argue. The man leaned in and hissed. "Go back to Bo-Dell-Win," he shouted, mangling the town name. "Wait for them as get leave to come use you."

Before she could object, a voice behind the guards demanded, "What is going on here, private?"

Both men stood a bit straighter. An older man peered at them from behind the gate. Finally the kinder of the two spoke. "This woman wishes entry to the camp, Sergeant. We told her no."

"Claims she's some soldier's wife," the other snickered.

The man studied Rosemarie carefully. She peered back;

something about him tickled her consciousness. "Who is your husband?" he asked.

"Lieutenant Henry Wheatly." She lied again with as much dignity as she could muster, and no little hope.

The sergeant's eyebrows rose. "Officer's wife? I think we can let this one in. Open that gate."

Rosemarie's heart gave a lurch. The gate was one barrier breached; the sergeant would be another. He gestured for her to follow. She skipped to keep up, determined to brazen it out if he took her to the authorities, hoping to at least talk to Harry.

"You're Harry's Rosemarie," the gruff old sergeant murmured without turning his head. She stopped in shock. "Keep walking," he hissed. "Look like you belong. Just follow me."

She did, and the man's name came to her. *McNaughton. Harry's McNaughton—it has to be.* He led her between to low wooden buildings and turned to face her. "Listen quick before someone asks questions. I'm leading you to the hospital."

He really is ill! Fear made her heart race. "How bad is he?"

"Bad enough. He was in and out for a while, but better now. Your voice will bring 'im round. He'd kill me if I don't bring you, but be careful. You can't lie forever."

"Take me to him, please." She tugged at his jacket, eager to run to Harry.

The man nodded. "They'll want papers, but we'll cross that when we come to it, do you hear? Just act like you belong."

He led her through a ward lined with beds and past a puzzled nurse to another room, one with only four beds. "Officers' ward," McNaughton shrugged.

A stern-looking nurse frowned at them. "Sergeant? Who is this?" she challenged.

"Harry!" Rosemarie gasped, dropping to her knees by his bed. He looked asleep. *So pale, and silent.* She reached a trembling hand to his cheek and found it warm, but not terribly so. Thickness clogged her throat at the overwhelming relief.

"She's the lieutenant's wife," Sergeant McNaughton said behind her back.

"I am unaware the lieutenant has a wife," the woman sniffed. Rosemarie heard her walk out of the room.

A coughing fit rising from deep in his chest seized Harry. Rosemarie put an arm under his shoulders and lifted him so he wouldn't choke. When he took a shuddering breath and leaned against her breast, she laid him down gently without waking him.

"How long has he been like this?" she asked, reaching for a cup at his bedside. She found it empty and frowned. "Isn't there water?" she asked.

McNaughton hunkered down next to her. "I've been fetching water. Empties the pitcher as fast as I bring it. How did you find us?"

She pulled out the letter she received. The sergeant whistled. "Took 'em long enough. Why dint you answer his letters?"

She stared at the man. "What letters?"

"He wrote to the priest in Amiens. He wrote to that cottage of yours. Lots of times. They all came back."

"Didn't he know I went to my cousin's farm when the fighting moved to toward the city? *Abbé* Desjardin knew, but he evacuated too."

"Is that where you've been?"

She nodded, her attention riveted on Harry. She took his hand in hers and leaned to kiss his mouth. "Harry, it's Rosemarie. I'm here. I love you."

His eyelids fluttered open, but before she could react, the nurse returned, an officer with her.

"There she is, Captain Mango. I have no record that the lieutenant has a wife, but this woman is here making claims."

Keeping one hand entwined with Harry's, Rosemarie gazed up at the man.

"I'll take care of it, Nurse Henderson," the captain said. His sympathetic gaze failed to take the sting out of his next words. "I'm sorry, ma'am, but do you have any proof of what you claim?"

Her heart sank to her stomach. *How could I have proof of a lie?*

"Rosemarie?" The voice from the bed drove all other thought away.

"Yes, my love, I'm here," she replied, kissing his forehead.

"Alive," he rasped, his familiar blue eyes scanning her face.

She choked on her laugh. "Very much so." She squeezed his fingers. "Oh God, Harry. I've been so frightened."

"Don't be," he whispered. "I'll take care of you." His eyelids drifted shut as if so many words had worn him out.

She didn't hear the captain leave, but Sergeant McNaughton must have followed because she could hear a muffled argument and then silence. She found herself alone with Harry.

Rosemarie laid her head on his chest with a sigh. "Get well, my love," she whispered. "I need you."

"Trying," he murmured sleepily. He said nothing more, but she felt his hand move to touch her hair. It was enough. Harry lived; he loved her. The even rise and fall of his chest reassured her that he slept peacefully, and all would be well.

She wasn't sure how much time passed; she may have dozed. Heavy footsteps brought her to attention. She turned to see the captain return with a sheaf of papers and an embarrassed expression, the stern-faced matron at his heels.

"I'm afraid we're going to have to ask you to leave, ma'am. We have a credible witness you're not his wife. His own father never heard of you."

Rosemarie stood clutching her hands together. She opened her mouth to object. *Surely they will let me stay and nurse him!*

The officer paid no attention. "The lieutenant himself told to the regimental clerk that he isn't married when he tried to reserve passage home for a wife—"

Rosemarie spun around to gaze at Harry. *Passage home? He means to take us!*

"—but we can't reserve berths based on what men intend, only on reality. There's a procedure. You can't just burst in here."

Rosemarie knelt again, flinging one arm over Harry. "They won't let me stay," she cried. He stirred but didn't waken.

"Please, ma'am," the captain said behind her. "You'll have to go home and wait."

"Harry, do you hear me? If they make me leave, I'll—" She had no idea what to do. She felt a gentle hand on her shoulder.

"Please," the captain said. "Come with me." He pulled her to her feet and out the door when she would have turned back. She didn't see Harry's eyes blink open.

Two guards waited to lead her out of the hospital toward the camp gate. Deflated and unable to defy such a show of force, she followed them down the dusty road past the headquarters building. She heard a shout and turned to see McNaughton running toward her, but he skidded to a stop when she neared the headquarters. Senior officers stood in front speaking with a tall man in a long civilian coat.

As her guards led her past, she heard the man complain, "I'm telling you my son isn't married," he said. "I would know. Throw the trollop out. I can take care of my son."

She tried to turn to him to beg him for help, but firm hands led her to the gate and closed it behind her.

CHAPTER 24

"Rosemarie," Harry croaked. He blinked again, forcing his eyes to focus, but saw no one. *Another damned dream? It had been so real. This time the army dragged her away,* he recalled.

His heart pounded against his chest as it did after a nightmare, but this time it was different. *She was real!* He would swear to it. "Mac," he called. He pushed himself up onto an elbow. "Mac!" he repeated as loudly as he could. Nurse Henderson appeared in the doorway, lips pursed and arms akimbo.

"The sergeant has been taken under guard. He has questions to answer." She fussed with the covers, and he batted her hands away.

"Fetch McNaughton!"

"Stop upsetting yourself, Lieutenant. Captain Mango has everything under control. That woman upset—"

"Where is she?" Harry demanded.

"I have no idea. The captain ascertained that she had lied her way in here, and she was escorted off base."

Harry pushed himself up, the movement making him dizzy. He held his head in his hands to right himself. The nurse put her hands on his shoulders to push him down, but he shoved them away with more force than either one of them knew he had.

"You must lie down, Lieutenant. I insist."

Harry staggered to his feet. "I'm going after Mac."

"Stop it! You are not well, and the general—"

"I don't give a tinker's dam about the general. I need to find Rosemarie."

He brushed past her and padded in his bare feet into the next ward. Light from the door blinded him temporarily before the bulk of a man filled it. Harry swayed on his feet.

"Mac, where the hell were you?" he asked just before his knees gave way and he hit the floor.

"My God, what is he doing out of bed? How incompetent are you people?"

It wasn't Mac.

Hands brought him to his feet and hustled him toward the bed over his feeble objections. Nurse Henderson's businesslike grip had the virtue of familiarity at least. His father's clumsy efforts to help brought rage and frustration up from his gut.

"Let me go, damn it," Harry demanded, thrashing around.

"Calm down, Harry," his father commanded.

Harry tried to fight his way back up, but weakness kept him pinned to the bed. He felt something stick into his thigh.

"That will calm him down, Mr. Wheatly," Nurse Henderson said, her voice sounding far away. "He needs to rest if he's to get well enough to..."

Darkness descended. Just before it did, Harry opened his mouth to wail "Rosemarie!" No sound came out.

Harry came awake slowly the following day, lying on his side and weighed down by the remaining effect of the drugs. He opened his eyes to peeling paint the exact color of his nightmares, muddy brown and drab. He closed his eyes against it. Rosemarie's face floated into memory, as it had many mornings before, only this time she leaned over him in this room.

She came! He rolled over with a gasp when a rustle to his back alerted him he wasn't alone. He prayed for Rosemarie's face, hoping it wasn't Henderson. Even Mac would be better. Someone else entirely sat by his bedside.

"Good morning, Harry," his father said. Harry fell onto his back and put an arm across his eyes to block the sight.

"Good to see you too," William Wheatly muttered under his breath.

"Where is she?" Harry demanded without moving his arm, or acknowledging the man who had come across the ocean to check on his wellbeing.

"The woman who broke in yesterday?" his father asked.

"Yesterday? I slept through the night?" he pulled down his arm and glared at his father.

"Yes. You're still weak, as your stupid stunt yesterday proved. They tell me you've come through the worst, however. Thank God. I wired your mother yesterday."

A niggle of guilt penetrated his fogged brain. "How is Mother?"

"Well enough but frightened for you."

The guilt settled in Harry's stomach. He would face it later. "Where's Rosemarie? They took her away, didn't they." It wasn't a question.

"She broke into a military facility without authorization. She could have been arrested."

Harry clamped his jaw shut to keep from screaming in frustration. He had proven he could not chase after her last night. He didn't care to repeat the humiliation.

His father didn't notice. "They let her go."

Their eyes held—Harry's dark with rage, his father's uncertain. The older man broke the silence eventually. "Sergeant McNaughton says the woman is important to you."

Understatement. "Where is Mac?" Harry snapped.

"He spent the night in the brig for smuggling a woman into camp. He's confined to quarters for a month."

Harry meant to send the sergeant in pursuit. He let forth a string of curses until he wheezed and had to stop for breath.

"The army hasn't improved your vocabulary," his father muttered.

"I must find Rosemarie. We have to marry quickly."

William Wheatly paled. "Have to marry? So that's it."

Harry swallowed hard, tempted to let his father keep his misconception. "Not what you think," he said. "If I don't get a marriage certificate soon, I won't get her a berth on a repatriation ship for months. We'll be stuck in Europe, or at least she will."

"That's ridiculous. You are in no position to support a wife. You have university—law school—a career to start. I can see you have an attachment to this woman. You'll get over it once you get home."

Harry narrowed his eyes at his father. "Actually staying over here would be my first choice. We can live in France, but I don't want to be separated for months until I can get free of the military." He saw no point of describing his fantasy: living with Rosemarie and Marcel at *les hortillonages*, her growing their food, Harry writing his novel.

The old man snorted and rolled his eyes. "Nonsense. You need to face up to your responsibilities. How will you earn your living?"

Five years of war, and the old man thinks I have to face up to responsibility? The fool has no idea.

"I'll grow wheat. It worked for Grandpa Matthews." The idea had some appeal. His mother's parents' home had been a refuge in his childhood, far from the city and the expectations laid on an only son by a demanding father. He wasn't about to tell the old man about his plan to be a writer.

"A life of backbreaking labor? Is that what you want?"

Harry refused to respond. "Get Mac," he demanded.

"I beg your pardon?"

"You're the Deputy-damned-Attorney General of the province. The brass will listen to you. Get Sergeant McNaughton sprung. I need him." His eyes bore into his father's.

It took all day, and the light through the west-facing window glowed orange when the sergeant walked into Harry's hospital room.

"Took you long enough. Did you get a pass?"

"Pass? I'm lucky to be out of quarters. Persuasive he might be, but it took your father all day to get me out. He had to go all the way to the general. The brass hats aren't happy. They hate it when civilians show up to throw their weight around. Told him so too."

Harry didn't have time to savor the image of a general giving his father a dressing down. "Get into the village and find Rose-marie. She'll have stayed there."

Mac shook his head sadly. "Your pa already sent men to ask. They couldn't find her."

"You go. You know what she looks like, and you know what to ask. We can't lose her now. Tell my father to get you a pass. He may as well push that authority he's so proud of around."

Mac shook his head mournfully. "I don't know, lad. I walked here as soon as they finished the big dressing down. Yelled at me instead of your pa. No good will come of it."

"Just do it. Find her Mac. Just find her."

Mac rose with a sigh and started for the door.

"And Mac—keep my old man out of here if you can."

CHAPTER 25

Rosemarie put a hand to her aching back and stretched her shoulders. Laundry work, difficult though it might be, at least kept her mind busy. Still, her thoughts ran in circles, images of Marcel alone at Remi's farm, memories of Harry sick with only that stone-faced nurse to care for him. She reassured herself that Elsa was a good mother and would care for Marcel. She reassured herself Sergeant McNaughton was loyal and would look after Harry. She had to believe they would be well; it became harder every day.

Her hands, hot and red from the work, ached when she plunged them back into the steaming tub. It had been kind of Mr. Pendall to give her work, even for a few days until his daughter-in-law returned. No one would hire her in Bodelwyddan, and she had to move on to Brynford to find work. She prayed the old harridan at the inn kept the message she left for Harry—or the sergeant if he came to check. At least she remained in Wales, only fourteen miles from Kinmel and the man she loved. She clung to that comfort.

Hours later she climbed to the cubby-hole under the eaves of the stables behind Pendall's inn. Ducking under the low ceiling, she reached up to the roof truss and pulled down the battered

valise that held her clean linen and paltry collection of treasures. She turned out her pocket and counted the day's pennies
before adding them to the sock she used to store her coins.
Pendall paid her enough to eat and still put a few back. If Harry
didn't come for her, she would have to pay passage back to
France, to Marcel.

He will come.

She considered writing to Elsa and decided not to spend the
postage. *Perhaps I'll have better news tomorrow.*

She pulled Harry's Bible, the concrete embodiment of his
love, out of the valise and shoved her fears into it along with the
sock full of coins. She lay on her pallet and hugged the book
close.

He will come.

BATHED AND DRESSED, Harry felt more himself. The fever had
abated three days earlier, and Mac had been gone two of those.
Harry determined he would be up and dressed when Mac
returned with word about Rosemarie.

His father haunted the base, irritating the general and driving
Harry mad. Harry refused to discuss Rosemarie and ignored the
elder Wheatly's everlasting nattering about Harry's responsibilities and so-called career prospects. Silence, he found, eventually
drove the old man to leave him alone.

He sat on the narrow bed, elbows on knees with his hands
clasped between them, considering his options when
McNaughton stomped in, William Wheatly hot on his heels.
Harry didn't have to ask. Mac's face told him all he needed to
know. He hadn't found her.

Harry's father, to his credit, listened quietly while Mac told
his story, how he managed to get the innkeeper in Bodelwyddan
to reveal that Rosemarie had to move on to another town—

Abergele he thought—to find work so that McNaughton could pursue her there. "That's what took the extra day."

Harry's stomach clenched when Mac shook his head and looked up at him, disappointment obvious in his expression. "Not there. She moved on to Brynford, but the work ran out, and she had to move again."

"What do you mean the work ran out?" Harry asked, even though he knew the answer in his gut.

"She has no money, Harry. She's working her way. I found the man who hired her in Brynford. Seemed to feel sorry, but he said he had no way to keep her on once his daughter-in-law returned. He only knew the direction she went, not whether she found work or not. It sounded to me like she's working her way back to the channel, heading home like."

Harry dropped his head to his hands, his entire body sinking under the force of disappointment.

His father's voice sounded like it came from a mile away, not just across the room. "The woman gave up and went home? She can't have been very steadfast. Probably for the best, Harry."

"You know nothing," Harry snarled, snapping upright. "Rosemarie Legrand has more backbone than anyone I know. You have no idea what she has endured these past years. You have no idea about—anything." He ended lamely, unable to spit out what he thought, that his father had no idea of the smell of death, the brown cloud of decay, or the hunger that eats at your belly. He knew nothing about what Harry had endured and less than nothing about a young mother raising a son with little food and fewer resources in a war zone. A niggle of guilt suggested his father knew nothing because Harry didn't tell him any of it.

"I know what's done is done," his father spat back before Harry could say more. "You may as well come home. The delegation sails from Liverpool in a week. You can come with us. I'm certain I can arrange it so you don't have to—"

"No! I'm not leaving without Rosemarie unless the army

tosses me on a repatriation ship, and even then I'll be on the first ship back."

"Don't be a damned fool. You can't just wander all over Europe. Come home. Get back to university. I'll hire someone to look for her in France." The old man's face lit up at that idea. "That's exactly what we should do, hire someone to find her." He sat back, smug in the belief he had neatly settled the matter.

You mean have her investigated while you sink your claws into me and bind me to your ambitions.

"Let me make this clear, Father. I love Rosemarie. I love her son Marcel. We may lack the formality of marriage, but they're my family. I will not desert them. I'm going after her."

"They won't give you leave to do that!" his father shouted.

"Don't try to block it. I'm going after her with or without leave."

William Wheatly blanched at the threat. Desertion was punishable by firing squad in time of war. The formal conflict may be over, but the army would not take kindly to absence without leave.

"Harry—" his father began.

Harry didn't wait to hear more. He rose to his feet, pleased to see how steady he was, and left with Mac on his heels. He had a pass to arrange.

CHAPTER 26

Pendall's eyes had been kind, but his position unshakeable when his daughter-in-law returned. "Sorry, lass. I can't pay both of you, and family comes first," he had said, leaving Rosemarie with no way to pay for room and board.

She tried to beg. "Is there any—"

"Not in Brynford, lass, but if you want to move on east, I know a man transporting goods to Dover."

Dover. East. Toward the coast and France, but away from Harry.

When she faced a choice between waiting—and hoping—for Harry while she starved or making her way back to France and Marcel who needed her, she had bitten her lower lip to keep from crying and nodded her head. When Pendall's friend offered her passage in exchange for loading and unloading at stops, her decision was made. Marcel needed her.

She slept under the wagon at night, and the drover had been kind, sharing his bread and purchasing soup for dinner. His kindness couldn't fill the hole Harry's absence left in her heart or calm her worries.

If only I had time to tell them about Remi's farm. If only Mac finds Pendall. If only...

The man left her in a tiny village above Dover, where he knew she might find work and the coin she needed for passage. The kindness of strangers had taken her so far. She prayed they would see her home safely to Marcel.

What then? She couldn't lean on Remi any longer. When she returned to the farm, she would fetch her son and return to Amiens to look for work. *Harry might come to find me in Amiens. Mac said he sent mail there before.* It was time to plant as well. People in *les hortillonnages* would already have lettuce to harvest. Growing things always soothed her soul. The more she considered it, the more the plan felt right.

A small fishery hired her. Rosemarie might have enjoyed the sea air if it wasn't buried beneath the smell of fish and charcoal. Still, cleaning fish for the smoker was easier work than laundry, and one of the fishermen agreed to transport her to France in the morning in exchange for her work. Again she didn't write to her cousins; she would reach them before a letter did.

She washed her hands under a pump and walked past the docks, then along the coast—trying to get clear of the stink, but bearing it with her. She stood on an outcrop where the wind might do its best to blow the smell of fish and the dark cloud of despair away.

Will Harry come for me? Did he get my messages? Will he know to come to Remi's farm? To the cottage? Dear God, she prayed, *let him come and find me.*

The sky darkened in the east, and the first stars began to twinkle.

Are you watching them, Harry? Follow the stars. Follow them home to me.

She turned and walked back to face a night on a pallet in the kitchen and her journey home.

～

Thirty damned days. Colonel Daniels would approve not one

day longer, and that grudgingly. "Go. At least it will get your father out of my hair. But I'm telling you—if a ship sails while you're gone, I'll drop you to the end of the queue, Wheatly. And if you're one day late, I'll have you up on charges, and McNaughton with you." He tossed the pass and another for Mac on his desk and slammed a drawer shut so hard the desk vibrated to show his disdain for impertinent lieutenants who asked special favors, particularly one with an interfering politician for a father.

Harry left within an hour with Mac on his heals. He didn't say good-bye to his father. They quickly found Pendall in Brynford, but he knew only that she had moved on east with a drover, and they used up six days of their leave eliminating every town within walking distance of Brynford in an effort to uncover her direction. His lingering weakness didn't help. When he almost collapsed after the third day, Mac threatened to tie him to a bed if he didn't slow down.

"Y'won't do the lass any good dead or as good as. If you want to find her you need to rest midday and sleep at night."

Harry forced himself to pause most days, but sleep at night wasn't always possible, not with Rosemarie alone somewhere in England working to survive. Guilt over his failure to protect her ate at him; frustration boiled inside. Even his attempts to keep ugly visions away by conjuring images of her little cottage in the floating islands failed to help. The place had been his refuge against the ugliness of war, one safe haven along the Somme. Now, the memory left him yearning and lost.

On the seventh day, they reached Chester, and hope flared when an innkeeper allowed as how a woman matching Rosemarie's description sought work.

"Unruly brown hair, the color of oak leaves?" Harry demanded.

"Don't know about no oak leaves. Brown's brown. Brown eyes too."

"Brown? I asked about hazel. Do they hint at green in some light?" Those eyes haunted Harry's dreams.

"I don't have time to peer into no ladies' eyes to see 'em change color. Told you it sounds like her. About so tall—up to my shoulder. Brown hair. Brown eyes. Had no work to offer so she moved on. That's all I know, and I have work to do if you'll get outta my way."

"One more thing—please!" The man turned back, frowning but attentive. "Did she mention France?"

"France? Why would she? Looking for work she was."

"She might have decided to return home."

"To France? You never said the woman was French. One I met were a Yorkshire lass clear as day." The innkeeper shook his head on the strange doings of Canadian lieutenants and wandered back to his taproom.

Harry's hope withered and died. He sank into a chair, leaned an elbow on the battered wooden table, and laid his head in his hand. Somewhere voices buzzed with cheer. A man's voice broke into song. "Pack up your troubles in an old kit bag and smile, smile, smile..." The crowd in the other room joined in while despair washed over Harry.

Mac sat down across from him, blessedly silent.

The innkeeper returned with two pints of ale, depositing them in front of the men. "You look like you can use this," he said gruffly, but without entirely masking his sympathy. He left as swiftly as he had come.

The ale and Mac's company raised Harry from his anguish. He pounded the table with his right fist. "I'm not giving up, Mac. I can't."

I will find her if it takes a year, Colonel Daniels's thirty days be damned. He sipped his ale, lost in thought, tossing around for a plan.

"A half dozen roads fan out south and east from here, and there must be a hundred inns between here and Dover—if she's going there. Folkestone may be more likely. Could even be Portsmouth," he speculated.

"We don't know as she would only find work in an inn. There are farms and stores—" Mac shrugged.

And plenty that would harm or exploit a woman on her own. Harry squelched the thought. "She might find passage across the channel in any fishing village on the coast as well."

"Needle in a haystack, Harry. We should head back to Kinmel. Let your da hire that investigator." Mac drained his ale.

"No! I'd rather eat nails than admit failure to that old man."

"But how're we going to find her?"

"We may not know her route, but we know where she'll go. At least we have a better chance at that. We have to go to Amiens."

"She wasn't there when you wrote," Mac reminded him.

"That was then. Where else would she go now?"

"Wherever she stashed her little fellow."

Marcel. Harry hadn't seen the boy in more than a year; his heart ached. *No wonder she couldn't linger long in Wales. Rosemarie will have left him somewhere safe, but where?* He shook his head. "Amiens is our one sure thing. They might have gone back, or if not, someone will know where they went. We're going back to Amiens."

Mac moaned dramatically. "If you say so, but I sure hoped never to see the bloody Somme again."

CHAPTER 27

Harry wondered if he'd acquired some sort of bad luck that rained disasters down on them after a broken axle, attempted theft, a bout of food poisoning, cancelled ferries, *mal de mer*, and a nasty bruised shin from walking on a pitching ferry. By the time the train from Dunkirk pulled into the remains of Arras and the stationmaster told him there would be no train to Amiens until morning, he was sure of it. He slept in fits and starts on a wood bench that night and left at dawn, Mac grumbling at his side. He'd ordered the sergeant back to camp twice, but the old curmudgeon stuck to him like a burr.

The station at Amiens, much the worse after four years of war, still managed to feel familiar. In spite of a constant drizzle, his pace picked up when the streets of the old city brought Rosemarie close in memory. The city had rallied to rebuild what had been lost, but the damage stirred his fears.

A thought stopped him in his tracks. *What happened to the islands? Is her cottage even there?* He had no idea and didn't plan to trouble Mac with his doubts. He refused to admit failure; he could not go back.

"The cathedral still stands," Mac said.

The ancient church loomed over the city, as it had for centuries, a beacon of hope to Harry as it had been for many.

"Aye. We'll start there." He had no idea if *Abbé* Desjardin, who had answered none of Harry's letters, was dead or gone, but he intended to find out. *Someone at the ancient parish knows where Rosemarie can be found.* He refused to believe otherwise.

They found the façade free of sandbags, Harry pushed the heavy door open, and they stepped out of the rain and into the gloom. Tall windows lined the soaring walls. Some, he noticed, were boarded over. The old place hadn't escaped damage entirely.

"Dark," Mac said.

Harry nodded but didn't reply; he walked briskly up the side aisle looking for a priest.

"Good place, though," the sergeant went on, keeping up with Harry. "Safe."

Harry bit back a bitter laugh. *Safe.* The old place was that, though hundreds of men—Canadian, British, French, Australian, New Zealander—even Yanks—had died to keep it so.

They wandered around the edge, circling the nave to pass a series of chapels, with no luck. Harry spun around and turned back. Mac followed Harry toward a small door they had overlooked at first. It was almost invisible, tucked as it was in the northeast corner of a chapel and dwarfed by soaring pillars and a massive painting of the Risen Christ above it. They took a few steps before it opened and a young—ridiculously young in Harry's opinion—man in a cassock came out. The priest stopped, eyes wide when he saw them.

"How may I help you?" he asked in English, eyeing their uniforms.

"I am looking for information about one of your parishioners," Harry replied in perfect French. "I'm looking for Rosemarie Legrand."

The priest shook his head sadly and responded more confidently in his own language. "There have been so many lost. That name is unfamiliar to me, but I have only been here a short while."

"Perhaps someone more senior—" *Someone older.*

The young priest didn't take offense. "Perhaps the *abbé* will recognize that name," he said. He turned back through the door and indicated they should follow, with a gracious gesture. They slipped out of the massive cathedral into a different world, a warren of sacristies and offices. When he led them to a small anteroom lined with closets, an older man turned from hanging vestments to peer at them curiously. He had a shock of silver hair and eyes so dark they looked black in the dim room.

"Harry! Thank the good Lord you've returned safely," the old priest exclaimed, clapping him on the back.

Thank Him indeed, Harry thought. *Abbé* Desjardin had returned as well. He explained his problems to the priest.

"So you see I had no idea you had written, or that you had not gotten Rosemarie's letters," the old man said, over steaming cups of coffee in his cozy sitting room in the rectory across from the cathedral.

"Good luck, us arriving the day after you returned," Mac murmured.

The *abbé* nodded. "Luck or providence," he said with a grin.

"But you haven't seen her?" Harry pressed. He leaned across the *abbé*'s table, his fingers tapping the edge of his cup.

"No, nor heard from her either. You say she traveled to Wales?"

"She did." Harry and Mac between described her visit, Harry's struggle with army regulations, and their efforts to find her. Harry left out his father's interference. He told the old priest about her need to work, simply to feed herself.

"We know she stopped to work periodically, but I thought she might be back here by now. She had more than a week's lead on us." Harry sank back in the chair, bleak despair weighing his body down. "I don't know where else to look."

The old man studied him carefully for long moments, sipping coffee, his shrewd eyes sharp. "Tell me, Harry, why are you so anxious to find her?"

Harry sat bolt upright. "To marry her of course!"

The old man smiled. "Does she know that?"

"Yes! Well, maybe not exactly. We never talked. I got pulled away, I wrote—" he cursed unapologetically. "Sorry father. The damned war," he murmured.

"The war, yes. A terrible thing. But, Harry, did you consider that the war brought you to Rosemarie?"

"And tore us apart. I have to find her. There's no time."

The *abbé*'s eyebrows rose. "The hurry of youth."

"True love is one thing," Mac responded, "and the army is another. He only has nine days left."

"Leave. I'm expected back in Wales, but I'm not going back until I find her."

"But you must go back, Harry. You can't help Rosemarie if you are arrested as a deserter."

"The war is over," Harry shouted, slamming a hand down on the table. "I did my damned duty. I'm not a deserter. I just need Rosemarie. I want to take her home." Images of his grandmother's kitchen rose in his mind. "If I can just find her and take her there, all would be well," he murmured.

"Need to get married first," Mac said. At the priest's knowing smile, he added, "He can't get her a berth on the repatriation ship without marriage papers. Army regulations."

The *abbé* laughed. "We don't want to interfere with army regulations." He eyed Harry. "So you intend to marry her, but you have to find her first. I have not heard from her since we evacuated eighteen months ago."

"She left the city?"

The priest nodded. "She needed to get Marcel away when the

fighting came so close. I knew she had a cousin with a farm a bit south of here, away from the front. She might have gone to him earlier for help, but he most likely struggled to feed his own brood of children. Only when the fighting reached the edge of Amiens did she swallow her pride."

"Where?"

The *abbé* wrinkled up his face, attempting to recall. "His name is Ronald... René... No! It is Remi Jacques. She wrote the directions down. I must have kept it, but so much happened quickly in all the chaos."

Harry almost choked on desperate hope when *Abbé* Desjardin rose and waddled to his desk to sift through papers and the detritus of a busy man's work. Harry followed the priest, peering over his shoulder at papers, holy cards, invoices, and envelopes.

The old man stood upright and shook his head apologetically. Harry's heart sank. They started back to the table, but *Abbé* Desjardin stopped in his tracks. "Wait!" he said bustling back to pull a metal box down from the top of his bookcase. He put it on the table and opened it. Another pile of notes lay inside, and this time he met success. He pulled one out and waved it in front of Harry's relieved eyes. It had the cousin's name and directions to his farm.

Moments later Harry and Mac stepped out into the plaza. "We need a car. Or a wagon. Anything to get us to this bloody farm." Sun peaked out between the clouds, and he blinked at the brightness.

"No guarantee she's still there," Mac pointed out glumly.

"No, but they may have word, or some idea where she is." Harry wondered if taxis still assembled on Rue de Fleurs and if any had survived the war.

He started in that direction when Mac called out. "Will you look at that?" Harry turned to the east where Mac pointed to see a double rainbow. Mac grinned. "Looks like our luck has turned."

I hope so, Harry thought. *We need it.*

CHAPTER 28

Rosemarie stumbled into her cottage without stopping to look at the signs of new life along her passage into *les hortillonnages*. The floating islands had sprung into late-spring glory, but she was simply too exhausted to care. She paid the boatman who docked next to her own little *barque à cornet*, neglected and half sunken, pushed open the unlocked door, and went inside.

Light, fading orange in the late afternoon, filtered through the window over the sink. She leaned her back against the door and surveyed the room listlessly. The window's curtains needed to be washed, and dust covered every surface due to her long absence.

Perhaps I'll clean in the morning before I leave. Perhaps not. She wondered if she ought to stay longer and rest before moving on.

Marcel needs me. Reminders of her son surrounded her. *I promised him Harry,* she remembered, tears welling up in her eyes. The little room filled her with memories of Harry as well: Harry laughing over dishes. Harry bringing flowers through the door. Harry playing with Marcel. *Harry,* a voice cried inside her, making her heart constrict in pain. *Has he been sent back to Canada yet, or does he still languish in that hospital?*

She pushed herself up and set her little valise by the narrow stairs that led to the tiny bedroom under the eaves. She fumbled inside it, pulled out the last of her bread and cheese, and set it on the battered wooden table. After fetching a cup of water, she sank down on a chair to eat.

In her mind's eye, she could see Harry sitting in the same chair, as he often had, usually with Marcel in his lap. Harry seemed to crave the little one's warmth even as she craved Harry's. *Was I a fool to fall in love with a soldier from the other side of the Atlantic?*

Harry frequently sat in the rocker in the corner, Rosemarie's one comfortable seat, where he held her so tenderly her cares fell away, and she felt dainty and beautiful. He had kissed her then, and his hands— *Oh, his hands!*

She shifted her eyes back to the table, but still memory flooded her. Sometimes Harry had used his grandmother's Bible, the battered old book that had brought them together, to teach Marcel.

The bread turned to sawdust in her mouth; she couldn't eat another bite. Harry said he would come for them when the war ended. He hadn't. She learned in Wales he never told his father about her either. The ancient story: a soldier loves in time of war, forgets when war ends. She had been a fool to believe it could be more.

She pushed herself up and took the remains of her meager meal over to clean up before bed. A bit of paper on the windowsill caught her eye, and Harry's signature grabbed her heart. She snatched it up.

I only got away for a day. Mac is covering for me. I'm glad you went somewhere safe. I'll come when the war is over.

Harry

He came looking for us! He'll come again, she thought, and she believed it this time. She thought of the Bible again. He had never taken it. He left it in her care, he said, "Because memories of this place have tied themselves to my memory of my grandparents' house," he had said. It kept him coming back.

She knelt down to open the valise next to the stairs and pulled out the book. A twinge of guilt twitched in her gut. She and Marcel had left in a panic, driven by the sound of guns, and she had almost forgotten the Bible. It had been Marcel who remembered.

Even if Harry didn't want us, he would have come for his Bible. She ran a hand over the book's leather cover, before carrying it to the rocker in the corner now lost in darkness.

She wrapped herself in the coverlet she kept in the chair, wishing Harry's arms held her instead of the soft fabric, hugged the Bible to her chest, and let tears fall until she fell asleep. Her last thought before sleeping was that she would clean the cottage in the morning. She would banish the ghosts of memory before she brought Marcel back. She would do that. *Tomorrow.*

THE TAXI WHEEZED up the lane to Remi Jacques's farm, bumping over ruts and swerving to avoid a roving goat until it spewed Harry and Mac out a hundred yards short of the house. The driver happily took Harry's money to wait. With or without Rosemarie, they planned to return to Amiens.

Mac followed Harry uphill toward the house where two boys chased each other around an ancient tree, laughing whenever one tagged the other and their direction reversed. The taller of the two stopped, and the other ran into him before turning to stare in the same direction as his companion.

As Harry approached, the younger boy grinned. "Harry!" Marcel threw himself at Harry, wrapping his arms around his hips.

"Goodness, Marcel, but you've grown a foot. I didn't recognize you at first." Harry sank to his knees and hugged the boy tight. "I've missed you!"

"I've missed you too, Harry, but where is *Maman*?" Marcel pulled away to look behind Harry as if his mother might be hiding back next to Mac.

Harry's heart sank to the ground. *She's not here.* Marcel's wide-eyed stare didn't help. Harry rose and took the little boy's hand in his.

Marcel peered up at him. The boy had hazel eyes—Rosemarie's eyes—and sadness clouded them. "She said she would bring you back with her. She promised."

"She went to look for me?" It wasn't really a question. "I've been looking for her, too. We must have missed each other."

The boy nodded vigorously. "But you will find her." Hope shone in his face, but Harry suspected fear lurked behind it.

A woman came to the door and wiped her hands on her apron. She bent to tell the older boy something that sent him off running toward the fields behind the house. Still holding Marcel's hand in his left, Harry removed his service cap with his right. "Good morning, madam," he said. "I am Lieutenant Henry Wheatly."

"Rosemarie's Canadian. You came for her. She said you would." Amazement and doubt reverberated in the woman's voice. "She isn't here."

Mac rambled up next to him, and her frown deepened. The sight of two tall soldiers in her yard seemed to disconcert the woman. Harry studied her weary face and worn clothing and wondered if she feared they would impose on her hospitality. "I gathered that," he said.

They stared at each other for an awkward space across a patch of weedy green. The return of the older boy broke the tension. Behind him a lean man with black hair and sparkling blue eyes approached.

"May I help you?" he asked, glancing between Harry and the woman in the doorway.

Before Harry could answer, the woman spoke. "Have you come for Marcel?"

I came for them both.

"You're Rosemarie's Canadian!" the man interrupted, unconsciously echoing the woman's words, but with excitement instead of suspicion. "Welcome to my home. I'm Remi Jacques, and this is my wife, Elsa. But where is Rosemarie? How did you find us on your own? And—listen to me talk. Come in. Sit. We will talk over tea." He gestured toward the house.

Elsa faded back into the house, and the men followed. Water simmering on the stove soon steeped tea in a pot on the table in the Jacques' sunny kitchen. Harry pulled Marcel into his lap, and the boy leaned his head on Harry's shoulder, filling one of the hollows in Harry's heart. He had missed the boy.

"There is no cake," Elsa murmured, looking embarrassed. "Would you like bread?"

Mac looked hopeful, but Harry didn't want to take from these people, remembering Rosemarie's struggles to feed herself and her son over the past few years. He and Mac could eat in Amiens. "No, thank you. Tea is fine," he said.

"Have you come from Rosemarie?" Remi asked.

Harry shook his head sadly. "Alas, no. I hoped to find her here." He and Mac explained to Elsa and Remi what had occurred in Wales and their efforts to find Rosemarie. "She has no money," Harry said, "She has been working as a laundrywoman to eat."

Remi shook his head. "I paid a fisherman to take her to England. I gave her what I could."

"I'm grateful to you. I don't know what she and Marcel would have done without you. We hoped she would have returned by now. I gather you've heard nothing from her."

"Not one word since she left," Elsa said from where she leaned against the sink.

"She has to be on her way here," Harry said. "She would want to hurry back to Marcel." He kissed the boy's head and sighed. "We've missed her somehow, and we're running out of places to look."

"And days to do it in," Mac growled, drawing a scowl from Harry who explained his pass to Remi.

Harry ran an agitated hand through his hair. "I don't know what to do next," he admitted.

"She will return here for Marcel," Remi said. "You could wait."

They could wait, but not there, if Elsa's frown meant anything. "Perhaps she's been delayed." Harry hoped Remi caught his meaning, not wanting to frighten Marcel with his worries about the sort of problems a lone woman on the road might encounter. Remi nodded.

"We have to return to camp," Mac said pointedly.

Harry didn't reply, but when Elsa produced a pencil and paper, he wrote the address out. "This will get to me through the army, but send word to the cathedral. *Abbé* Desjardin will know what to do."

"Will you take Marcel with you?" she asked.

"I can't."

"I want to go with you Harry," Marcel insisted. A fierce longing to keep the boy close almost overran Harry's common sense. He realized with a sinking heart that he had no place for the boy as long as he still searched for Rosemarie.

"I'll come back for you as soon as I find your mother, Marcel. For now I have no way to care for you, and if I go back to camp"— he said *if*, not *when* —"I can't have a boy with me."

Marcel turned his face into Harry's shirt, but he said nothing. His stoic endurance of difficulty grieved Harry. Until he found Rosemarie, he could do nothing for the boy.

Harry and Mac rose to leave, but Harry took Remi aside and handed him what money he could before departing. Remi tried to refuse, but Harry insisted in spite of a fierce frown from Mac. "For her passage to England, and your care for Marcel," he said.

Not long after, he let Marcel follow him to the waiting taxi for a final hug.

"I'll be back," he whispered.

"I hope you didn't give away your passage back to Wales," Mac grumbled as soon as the taxi bounced out onto the main road.

"I did not, but there isn't much more than that. You best leave tomorrow if you plan to eat."

"Six days left. If we leave tomorrow, we should get back in plenty of time, even if we hit a delay."

"I said 'you,' not 'we.'"

"You bloody fool. They'll bring you up on charges if you don't go back on time." Mac argued all the way back to Amiens.

"The army be damned. I'm not going anywhere without Rose-marie and Marcel. I left enough in my account to get them a room in Bodelwyddan until they can sail. We'll manage." *As long as it doesn't take more than a month or two.*

"Not if you're in the brig," Mac muttered under his breath.

After a night in the pilgrim's hostel near the cathedral, thanks to the good graces of *Abbé* Desjardin, Mac emptied his pockets, keeping only what he needed for passage and adding a few pounds to Harry's store. "No use to me," he said with a straight face. "You'll have to get someone to convert them to francs."

Harry took the gift gratefully and walked him to the train, but he couldn't think of anything else to say.

With Mac gone, Harry found himself at loose ends with nothing to do but wait. He didn't want to trail after the *abbé* like the lost sheep he undoubtedly was. He tried sitting at the train station watching for arrivals, but service continued to be sporadic and unpredictable, and he couldn't be certain she would come by train. Wandering led him inevitably to the old medieval quarter and the river.

Staring at lilies growing along the bank, he saw boatmen coming and going. He'd hired them often enough to take him to Rosemarie's cottage. As long as Marcel resided at Remi's farm, that would be Rosemarie's first destination, and for that reason, he had early on dismissed the cottage as a place to search. He still doubted she would go there, but with nothing else to do, he decided to check. It would at least be a quiet place to spend the night.

A boatman agreed to take Harry out but insisted he had to sell his produce first, and Harry sat on the quay to wait and just stare at the river. The blue of the current looked unfamiliar. Harry remembered the Somme running brown with mud and, he suspected, blood as well. Harry knew that less than a mile upriver the banks would be bare of all vegetation after four years of armies marching back and forth, clawing forward from trench to trench. He wondered idly if nature had time to reassert itself in the six months since the armistice, but he had no desire to find out. The island had been his refuge. To the island he would go.

The boatman poled his *barque* skillfully in and out the canals between islands. They came around a bend and Rosemarie's island, overgrown and untended, loomed in front of him. Fears for Rosemarie stifled the joy of homecoming until he saw a light flicker in the window, and a surge of hope made his heart race.

CHAPTER 29

R osemarie lit the candle by the sink and another on the table. It wasn't quite dark, but she needed to repair a blouse. Her little valise lay next to the door because she planned to leave at first light, eager to go back to Marcel. She had been wise to stay overnight. The rest had done her good, and arriving in Elsa's kitchen too exhausted to move would have been a mistake.

She hummed a little as she stitched until a sharp knock on her door interrupted the quiet of the islands. She dropped her mending, raised a shaking hand to her chest, and rose to her feet.

Who on earth would come out here? Who knows I'm here? She put an ear to the door warily but jumped back shocked when the doorknob moved. She took a step farther back as the door slowly opened.

He stood bathed in the light of sunset, his eyes full of joy. "Rosemarie! Thank God. I was afraid some stranger—"

She cut off Harry's words when she threw herself into his arms, stood on tiptoe, and covered his mouth with hers. With his arms clamped around her, one hand slipped under her bottom, and he lifted her off the ground to deepen the kiss. When she pulled back to take a breath, he let her slide to her feet but kept her in his arms. Still unable to speak, she ran her fingers over his face as if to verify he was her Harry. He kissed her fingers when they touched his lips.

"You're here," she breathed at last. "How?"

"I didn't think you'd be here," he said at the same time.

She pulled him in and shut the door, both of them talking at once. He hugged her again and kissed her thoroughly while her heart sang. *Thank God, thank God, thank God.*

When they moved to the rocker and he pulled her into his lap, they began to tell their separate stories of travel, confusion, and longing, with frequent interruptions for questions and repetition punctuated by kisses. Words gave way eventually, and kisses took their place.

Much later, the practical French housekeeper in Rosemarie surfaced briefly. "Are you hungry? There is little here…"

"Food isn't what I hunger for," he replied, his smoldering look sending tremors through her belly and feminine parts. She melted into his heated kiss. This time Harry pulled back. "If you need to eat, though, I could take you into Amiens for dinner," he said, concern driving desire from his eyes.

She shook her head. "My *barque* is low in the water. It is too late to bail it out. And I have what I need here," she said, sliding her hands into his hair, kissing his forehead, and moving her mouth down to nibble his ear. She smiled against his skin when she felt his kisses on her neck. When his hands roamed up her back and down over her breast to caress her belly, her breathing came in gasps.

"Rosemarie," he whispered against her mouth. "We will marry tomorrow."

She sat upright, startled. "Marry? Tomorrow?"

His hands clamped on her waist and held her in place. "I'm sorry. That wasn't a very romantic proposal, but we talked about it before, and I hoped you—"

"Of course I'll marry you, foolish man—but tomorrow?"

"I have no time, Rosemarie. I could be in serious trouble if I don't go back, but I'm not going without you and Marcel. *Abbé* Desjardin understands. He'll marry us quickly."

She scanned his face. *Of course I'll marry him—but immediately? Aren't there practical details?* She couldn't think what they were.

"Besides, we have to have the papers," he added earnestly.

"Papers?" She was thoroughly confused now.

"The army wants papers. So I can arrange a ship for you and Marcel." He studied her avidly. "To come home with me to Canada. Am I getting ahead of myself again? I just— I need to take you there. To meet my mother and grandmother. We can come back here if you want, but I need to take you home first."

Too startled to reply, she stared at him. He had talked about Canada many times. It sounded wonderful.

Little keeps me here as long as I have Marcel and Harry.

"Please Rosemarie. I love you more than life itself. Just trust me. We will figure it all out."

She leaned in, open mouthed, and kissed him as thoroughly as she could. "Yes," she whispered. "I do trust you."

Fire flared in his eyes. "We'll be wed tomorrow," he said hoarsely.

She understood then. He had pleasured her many nights in that chair while Marcel slept above them, but he had never completed the act, lack of comfort and privacy being fierce chaperones. They would be husband and wife soon enough. In God's eyes, they were already.

She gave his mouth one more swift salute and stood, pulling him with her. In answer to his unspoken question, she took his hand and led him to toward narrow stairs.

"Wait!" he said. He blew out the candles, latched the door, came back to her, and scooped her into his arms before she could move, lowering his mouth to hers. He loved her. No words were needed. He carried her above stairs; they had a night to show each other just how much love passed between them before the world and its troubles crowded in again.

~

HARRY PULLED the little boat from the canal and tipped it to empty out the water shortly after dawn, a smile of pure bliss glowing across his face. It was, he thought, the first morning of the rest of his life without war or uncertainty to plague him. Memory of her lovely face against the pillow in the early morning made his heart swell as if it would burst.

Close examination of the bottom of the boat revealed no leak. If there had been one and they had been forced to linger a day to make repairs, his joy would only increase. In fact, the thought of staying tempted him, but he could not. He picked up the rag he had collected earlier and cleaned the seats as best he could. The little *barque* would serve as their wedding barge; he could at least remove the dirt.

Lilies bloomed at the water's edge, and Harry couldn't resist plucking one to bring in, but he left the rest so they would be fresher if she wanted a bouquet. He went in and found Rosemarie descending the stairs wearing a simple blue dress, cinched at the waist where a line of pearl buttons ended, the sort of dress she would wear for a feast day. He gaped at her, caught between his delight in her appearance and his worry that she might wish for something more elegant.

When she smiled in a way that curled round his heart and walked closer, he noticed that she carried a bundle of lace over one arm. "What is this?" he asked, longing to take her in his arms, but careful not to touch her or the lace with his work-soiled hands.

She took the lily from him. "My grandmother's *châle*. I saved it for our wedding."

"A shawl—a veil to cover your head," he grinned down at her, delighted at her preparations and happy she owned at least one beautiful thing for their wedding, rushed though it might be.

She twirled the lily between the fingers of one hand. "Are there more of these?"

"Yes! And the *barque* is sound. We'll have no problem leaving this morning."

A flash of regret marred her features. "We might have stayed."

His longing to embrace her, dirt and all, intensified.

We could—but no.

It was imperative they marry and return to Wales with all speed if he wanted to get them on one of the repatriation ships.

"You will outshine me this morning. Let me get cleaned up, while you finish packing," he said instead.

The sun rose above the city as they wound through the canals and out into the river on their way to their wedding. Harry frowned when they pushed out into the main channel. *The bloody damned Somme, source of all my pain, route of my greatest joy.*

Rosemarie didn't notice his abstraction, and he tried to keep his eyes on the massive church soaring above the old medieval buildings to focus on what was to come. In the end, he lost the battle, his eyes drawn irresistibly upriver. Visions of mud, of trenches, and of the mangled bodies of men rose up to blind him. For a moment he wandered the battlefield, lost and alone, across the devastated landscape.

"Harry?" His soon-to-be wife's voice cut through his flashback, her concern flowing through him like healing balm. It was then that he heard it, the sound of a trumpet. He heard *The Last Post*, the slow and mournful salute to the dead, as clear as if the trumpeter sat beside him in the boat. He looked back upriver just as the final notes floated through him and saw the spring flowers sprouting along the bank, life regenerating out of the chaos.

He turned back to Rosemarie. The war had ended. He didn't know if he would ever exorcise it from his soul, but it had ended.

"I'm well," he told her, and looking at her precious face, he knew it was true.

CHAPTER 30

They surprised *Abbé* Desjardin over his breakfast. When the housekeeper escorted them in, he beamed at them. At the sight of the lace over Rosemarie's arm, his eyebrows shot up momentarily before he shrugged and laughed. "Harry warned me his time was running out. But surely you have time for coffee and a croissant?"

They obliged the old priest, although Harry's stomach threatened to rebel. Rosemarie picked at hers while the *abbé* studied her. Harry suspected the priest wanted to be sure she wasn't being pressured. She was—by circumstance, not by Harry—but her happiness seemed obvious. The priest must have been satisfied. He rose, brushed crumbs from his cassock, and asked Rosemarie where she wished to stand for the ceremony.

Harry hadn't considered that. He watched the two consult and followed where they led. As they walked up the transept and past the choir, the high altar of Notre-Dame d'Amiens, built to impress the masses, overwhelmed him. He wondered what his Methodist grandmother would think of the place.

Rosemarie led him toward the back of the cathedral. They passed a side chapel with a gaping hole in its wall from shelling, one of the few badly damaged parts of the church, and stopped at apex of the apse. The walls of the Virgin Chapel remained intact, but some of its lofty windows lacked glass. Luckily they hadn't been boarded up, and sunlight still flowed into the space. Smaller and more intimate—if a chapel with walls a hundred feet high can be called intimate—it suited his bride.

While *Abbé* Desjardin unlocked the ornate iron gate, Rosemarie paused and arranged her grandmother's lace masterpiece over her hair. She took Harry by the hand to lead him to the altar, her face solemn. The young priest Harry had met before and the abbé's housekeeper trooped in behind them to serve as witnesses.

They stood in front of a small altar beneath a statue of a woman holding a toddler on one hip who appeared to gesture to Harry with her other hand as if to invite him to come closer. When he saw the same welcome in Rosemarie's eyes, he couldn't look away. Her eyes held him while they repeated the ancient vows that bound them together, promising to honor, to cherish, to love. Harry's entire life force centered on the words and the woman, and he knew they would always be his truth.

A clearing of a throat brought him back to awareness. The *abbé* asked him something. "A ring, Harry? Did you have time to get a ring?"

He hadn't. "I'm sorry, Rosemarie. I'll get you one when I can."

She smiled. "Foolish man, I care nothing for that," she whispered.

It was done, and Harry stared into his beloved's eyes, unable to move until laughter reminded him of his duty. He kissed her, well and thoroughly.

When they adjourned to the *abbé*'s study to sign papers, they discovered the housekeeper had conjured up a delicious cake— although, being French, "cake" was perhaps too simple a word. The multilayered concoction was frosted and filled with berries; Harry discovered his appetite had been restored. He happily munched on a second piece while Rosemarie signed multiple copies of her marriage certificate.

"We will satisfy your army's need for triplicate and paper-work, no?" the old man said, folding each carefully and putting them in an envelope. "What will you do now?"

"Collect Marcel," Harry replied.

"How many days do you have left?" the *abbé* asked, throwing cold water on Harry's heated fantasies of lingering at the cottage.

"Four. Perhaps three."

HOWEVER MUCH HER husband wanted a speedy departure, they couldn't simply leave Amiens. Rosemarie insisted they visit the *mairie,* the town hall, to repeat their vows for legality and then the recorder of deeds so she could sign over her cottage and its furnishings to Remi. She owed him that much.

An old man who remembered her father agreed at buy her *barque.* Harry fetched a taxi and saw to the loading of her bundles, while they waited for the old man to fetch cash to pay her. Harry didn't complain, but she could feel his body tensing as a precious hour ticked by. He went off to send a telegram to Mac alerting him that they were on their way—and married.

The man returned as he promised, however. When she offered the proceeds from the sale of her boat to Harry, he pushed it back to her. "Put it away and keep it safe. We may need it before our journey ends, but you keep it for now."

She complied. It was little enough, but it pleased Rosemarie to bring something into her marriage. "He promised more in the fall," she told him.

He put an arm around to pull her close while the taxi made its way out of the city to bounce down ever-smaller roads until it wheezed once again up to Remi's farm.

Harry jumped out, and Rosemarie hung on to his hand to steady herself, her attention riveted on the little house and the boy running down hill.

"Maman!" Marcel shouted, flying into her embrace. She swung him around and hugged him until he wiggled to get free, talking happily. "Harry came with his friend Mac, but you weren't with them, and Harry said he would go find you, and he did," Marcel burbled and grinned at Harry. "He promised, and he did."

The boy twisted sideways when Harry ruffled his hair. "How fast can you pack your things?" Harry asked.

Marcel spun around to look at his mother. She glanced up at Harry. "We have news," she said. Before she could explain, Elsa and Remi approached. "Perhaps we'd best sit down first, and then I will tell you everything," Rosemarie said. She pinned her eyes on Harry, hoping he understood they couldn't just grab the boy and run off.

"The taxi—" Harry began, but Remi interrupted to assure them he would take them to the coast. Harry capitulated with good grace and went to pay the man. Soon they all crowded around the table in Elsa's kitchen, Marcel in Harry's lap. Remi peppered them with questions, and Elsa bustled about making tea.

Facing her cousins while Harry waited silently, Rosemarie wished she had taken time to talk to Marcel before being hustled into the house. She groped for words before simply blurting, "We're married."

The room went silent, all eyes on Rosemarie, but hers on her son. Marcel blinked at his mother before turning to look at Harry. "Married," he whispered wide-eyed. "Does this mean you're taking my mama away?" Her heart lurched.

Harry hugged the boy close. "It means I'm taking both of you with me," he said. "It means we're family now, Marcel." The boy clung to him, too overcome to speak, and Rosemarie blinked back tears.

She wouldn't have heard Marcel if he had spoken. The room exploded in a burst of congratulations, everyone clamoring to be heard. Cookies Elsa had claimed she had forgotten suddenly appeared, and she insisted on serving them to celebrate, while Remi demanded every detail.

Neighbors were sent for, and the conversation wandered in several directions as folks added their stories of their own to the wishes and excitement. Rosemarie struggled to be patient when people began to recall earlier weddings. She glanced at her husband often, worried that strangers and delay made him uncomfortable, but he seemed deep in conversation with Remi.

Darkening shadows of late afternoon worried her, especially when evening neared and it became clear there would be no travel that night. When Elsa insisted the boys could sleep in the kitchen because "newlyweds need their privacy," Rosemarie ran out of arguments not to stay. She reached for Harry who earned her gratitude with a kiss.

"Privacy is a gift we can use, wife," he whispered against her ear, making her cheeks burn. The warmth of his smile filled her, but he didn't quite mask his concern. Rosemarie knew Remi's hospitality would save them the cost of an inn. A trip across the channel on that fisherman's sailboat would cost less than the ferry as well. They were saving money, but time, an even more precious commodity, slipped through their fingers at an alarming rate.

CHAPTER 31

Tide and elusive wind delayed them much of the next day, but when the fisherman finally maneuvered his boat out of the cove in the late afternoon, a fair wind, England bound, blessed them.

"So you found your man," the fisherman had said in greeting, recognizing Rosemarie. Remi told the truth. The man was gruff, but kind, and he charged far less than the ferry. "Have to go out 'n fish, don't I?" He had grumbled. He left Harry and Rosemarie their privacy at the bow and patiently answered Marcel's questions at the stern.

The sound of the craft's small sail snapping into place reassured Harry they would make good time. He tipped his head up to the sun, sinking toward England as it was, and reveled in the wind at his back. From her expression, Rosemarie loved it as well. He reached out a hand and entwined their fingers.

"The wind was a stroke of luck," Harry said when they climbed out well before dark.

"Luck or Providence?" Rosemarie asked, failing in her effort to look stern.

My mother and grandmother are going to adore this woman. When a boy with a cart appeared, eager to help them transport their bags, he was certain luck—or Providence—was on his side.

Harry carried Marcel, boneless from sleep, up the hill into town, and down the cobbled street of a village the man called Dare. His confidence lasted until they reached the train station. The village where they had arrived had a train depot as the fisherman had assured them. It also boasted one main road and few side streets. Harry hadn't considered that such a place may not have frequent—or even daily—connections.

"Tomorrow noon, sir, sure's the sun comes up," the man behind the ticket window assured him. No amount of urgent prodding produced another option. Hiring a wagon to the next town merely put them on the same line. They had to spend the night where they were.

Putting his most reassuring smile in place, Harry turned to Rosemarie. "Tomorrow it is," he said, waving their tickets before stuffing them in his jacket. "Let's find some dinner and a place to sleep tonight." He prayed he didn't have to ask her for the proceeds from her *barque* this quickly.

Leaving them to clean up for dinner, Harry went down to ask the innkeeper if he could send a telegram to Kinmel Park.

"From Dare, sir? You'll have to do that when you get where you're going. We've a phone line at the post office," the man said proudly, "but it went down last week, and they haven't come to fix it."

What can't be fixed must be endured. Thank God I telegraphed Mac from Amiens. He knows we're on our way.

It would have to be enough. Harry went up to escort his family to dinner.

Marcel perked up when presented with a steaming bowl of stew. "Meat, Maman. Big pieces!" He tucked in with enthusiasm while Harry swallowed lumps in his throat and resolved the boy would never go hungry again. Once the boy finished every crumb of the pound cake that followed the stew, Marcel jumped down to chat with a boy on the porch of the inn overlooking the harbor and his new passion, sailboats.

As soon as he was out of earshot, Harry's new wife leaned in to peer at him sharply. "How much trouble are you in?" she demanded.

"What do you mean?" Harry temporized.

"I've counted the days. Can that train leave here at noon and get you to Kinmel Park before midnight tomorrow?"

No, especially since the last ten miles are by omnibus. He estimated them to be at least two full days from Bodelwyddan. "No. I'll be late."

Her voice dropped to a strained whisper. "Will they think you are a deserter?"

She must be terrified. They shoot deserters in time of war—but the war is over. "Nothing so dramatic. More like a malingerer. We'll do the best we can, and I'll throw myself on the mercy of the colonel. I may do a day or two in the brig." *Or months. Or be fined. Or discharged without separation pay or benefits.* "He's a reasonable man."

She didn't seem satisfied, but she didn't ask more, keeping her worries to herself.

Late in the night when he held his sleeping wife in his arms and his new son slumbered peacefully on a cot in the corner, Harry gave his fears full rein. He had enough saved to keep them for a couple of months, but he counted on separation pay to support them for at least the first half year. If they sentenced him to prison, it could be months before he was free.

Staring at the rafters, he could no longer avoid a distasteful conclusion. He would have to see his father and beg. Father would take in Harry's wife and see to Marcel, but the remaining question turned Harry's stomach: what will he demand in return? He knew the answer: law school—Father's dream not Harry's, the weight that loomed over his teens and his two years at university. Now it appeared Harry might have what he wanted most—Rosemarie and Marcel—at the cost of long dreary years clerking in his father's office. Had he survived the Somme for that?

Rosemarie stirred in his arms, murmuring something incomprehensible. He kissed her tenderly. "Go back to sleep. There is no rush in the morning. She snuggled in closer, and certainty filled him. He would do whatever he had to do. As long as he had this woman's love, he could do anything.

As it turned out, they arrived in Bodelwyddan in the late afternoon of the third day, two later than Harry was supposed to report. Mac had done his job, obtaining rooms at the Blue Goose Inn and paying a month in advance, adding to Harry's debt. The innkeeper had the grace to look shamefaced at Rosemarie. Neither mentioned the woman's inability to give her work when she had been there before. He welcomed them as honored guests and led them up to two rooms, "our finest," on the upper floor.

They watched Marcel bounce on the bed in the adjoining room astonished to find he had a room to himself. Harry felt a smile spread at the sight. *The boy will thrive in Canada*, he thought. *In peace*, he corrected.

"You must go quickly," Rosemarie urged, as if a few moments could make a difference.

He took her in his arms and kissed her thoroughly, knowing it might have to do for a while. He glanced into the other room, and seeing Marcel pay no attention, he deepened the kiss, pouring his passion into it.

"Rosemarie, I'm sorry. This isn't what I hoped. I probably won't be able to come to you," he began. "At least not for—"

She silenced him with a quick kiss. "Do what you need to do. Do not worry about Marcel and me."

What did I do to deserve this woman? He kissed her again, until she gasped for breath. "I'll send Mac with word. Count on it."

She gave him a little push. "Go. Do what must be done. We'll wait."

CHAPTER 32

Rosemarie put her fears firmly aside. Harry intended them to stay in this place for several weeks. She would make it a home for Marcel as best she could, and if God was kind, Harry. The little room had a bed big enough for two; a tall dresser, much too spacious for the few belongings she had been able to bring; and a lovely vanity with a mirror and bench.

She opened her bundles and began to put her clothing away in the dresser. Harry's Bible lay at the bottom of her valise. She took it to the vanity where he would see it when he came. She ran a loving hand over the warped old book. A hairbrush and some female whatnots joined it.

Her eyes strayed to the other piece of furniture, an upholstered rocking chair, lumpy and worn. Tears stung her eyes. She didn't miss much in her cottage among the islands, but she wished for her rocker.

"Maman?" Marcel sounded concerned. She swiped at her eyes and smiled at the boy.

"I am well, Marcel, just tired." She resolved that once they settled in their own home she would make sure the first piece of furniture they obtained was a rocking chair, one big enough for a man to hold his wife in his lap.

She helped Marcel unpack his shirts and underthings into the small dresser in his room. They piled his three books on a bedside table by the lamp. His biggest treasure, the model *barque* Harry had made for Marcel the first Christmas, had place of honor on the top. Marcel had protected it through war, evacuation, and life in a house full of rowdy cousins.

"Do you suppose this town has a public pond? A park perhaps? You could sail your *barque*. Let's look in the morning."

Too weary to explore that evening, they went down to dinner. She had been assured meals were included in their fare. The luxury to her wasn't the food; it was watching her son eat his fill with no restriction.

Upstairs, she pulled her son into bed with her and began to read to him. Though married less than a week, she dreaded sleeping alone. Without Harry, her heart felt hollow. She began to list ways she would make a home for him when they were able.

Please God, make it soon.

A knock on the door sent her hopping to her feet, one hand on her heart. Harry had only been gone two hours or three. If Mac came so soon, it must be bad news. The door opened before she could reach it.

"Harry! What—"

He had her in his arms and the air knocked out of her before she could think, spinning her around and scooping up Marcel to join them in the improvised dance. They all dropped on the bed dizzy and laughing.

Marcel scrambled to his knees. "Do it again, Harry!"

Harry's laughter healed her fears. "Maybe later, Marcel," he said. "First, I have news."

"Please!" Rosemarie said. "Why are you back so soon? I would fear bad news if you weren't so full of nonsense."

"Now I don't know where to start."

"The beginning usually works," she said primly. "Start there."

He did. Her shock almost matched his when she discovered he had been honorably discharged during his absence.

"Remember I told you about my father's demands."

"He said you had no wife. He didn't lie." Rosemarie had never faulted the man.

"That was my fault for never telling him. I just stopped answering his letters."

"That is very bad of you! He's your father." *No one should dishonor their father.*

"He just didn't want to listen when I tried to tell him I did not want to follow him into law and politics. I stopped arguing and began closing him out when I was very young."

"But what does that have to do with the army?" She had lost the thread of the story.

"Apparently he threw his weight around. He didn't listen to me about that either. I never wanted his influence. I never wanted him interfering."

"He arranged an honorable discharge?"

"Yes!" he took both her hands in his. "He did! For once I'm glad he ignored my wishes. I'm separated from the army with full pay. We can go home."

She kissed him quickly. For a moment, joy pushed all thought aside, but not for long. "But will the army still transport us to Canada?"

"They might, I don't know. It doesn't matter though. This is the best part." He reached in his jacket, pulled out a wrinkled envelope, and handed it to her.

"From your father?" she asked, staring down at the envelope addressed to Lieutenant Henry William Wheatly, puzzled by his meaning.

He grabbed it back. "Let me read it."

Harry,

By now you have returned to Kinmel Park. I hope you found

your Rosemarie and brought her with you. I had no idea how much she meant to you or for how long.

"See. You should have told him," Rosemarie chastised.

"Probably. But hush. Let me finish."

There is much we should say to each other, and I pray we get the chance. By now you know I've interfered in your life again. Try to forgive me. I'm attempting to make things up to you.

The army will have told you that you have been released from service and are free to go. You are also free to stay, Harry. Go to France and find her if you haven't already. Stay in France if you must, but I hope you don't.

Come home, Harry, at least long enough for us to meet her and the little fellow. Come to reassure your mother and grandmother that you are well. Then go live your life as you please. You'll find funds in your account sufficient to book first-class passage for your new wife and son. She deserves it.

I love you, Son.

Your father

PS

The *Croix de Guerre*, Harry? You didn't tell me that either.

Silence filled the little room, Harry expectant, and Rosemarie too stunned to speak.

"Will we go to Canada now?" Marcel asked.

Rosemarie and Harry laughed simultaneously.

"Yes!" Harry said.

He looked like a man who had been offered a fortune, but Rosemarie didn't think they had any such thing. "First class?" she mused. "That is not wise. What will we save if we travel more frugally?"

"What is this, my practical wife?"

"We have a home to make, Harry, and furniture to buy."

Warmth grew in her chest, and she knew he must see it in her eyes. "I want a rocking chair."

Laughter bound them together at that. "Me too," he replied.

In the end they compromised on a second-class cabin with an alcove for Marcel. The boy enjoyed walking the decks of the massive steamer that took them to Montreal. He enjoyed the attention of the returning Canadian soldiers who escaped their berth in steerage to walk the decks as well. He enjoyed dinner in the dining room.

Harry enjoyed their passionate—but quiet—nights in the narrow bed of their cabin, and he enjoyed their walks under the stars after Marcel slept even more, seeing the stars together at last.

EPILOGUE

The farmhouse came into sight when they turned the bend by the big old maple. Harry could make it out, familiar and lit in welcome, through the driving snow. He grinned at Rosemarie beside him in the sleigh, wrapped so thoroughly in woolens and fur that only her eyes and nose poked out. Of Marcel he could see even less, the boy having made his own den of blankets at their feet right after they pulled out of Humboldt in the rented equipage.

The lane to the farmhouse had been shoveled. Grandfather's hired man, Martin, and Harry's Uncle David were hard at work cleaning the steps.

"We're expected," Harry grinned, bringing the sleigh to a halt.

"The conquering hero!" his uncle exclaimed, clapping him on the back "You best get in there before your mother and grandmother explode. We'll deal with the horses."

Harry lifted Rosemarie from the sleigh and set her down quickly so he could catch Marcel, who launched himself into his new father's waiting arms. They climbed the steps, and Rosemarie clutched his arm a bit tighter as they approached the door. Under the shelter of the porch roof, he removed his hat to shake off the snow while they stomped the ice from their boots and Harry brushed snow from Rosemarie's shoulders.

"They will love you," he whispered just before the door flew open, and affection, cries of joy, and the scent of cinnamon and cloves engulfed them.

Rosemarie was soon seated with his mother and grand-mother by the iron stove. His mother had an arm around her shoulders, and Grandmama was offering a mug of warm spiced cider. Rosemarie and his mother had bonded when they first arrived in Regina from Montreal, but this was Grandmama's first meeting. Rosemarie understood how much this place and the people in it meant to Harry. She wanted to visit as soon as they reached Canada, but practical arrangements had taken longer than expected.

Grandfather brought Harry warm cider and love, but he, too, drifted over to meet the bride. Harry was left surrounded by aunts, cousins, and a familiar neighbor or two, who peppered him with questions. He looked around for Marcel but needn't have worried. David's boys had him well in hand and led him toward the kitchen. Harry longed to follow.

He sidestepped questions about war, well aware that, while people at home thought they wanted to know, they didn't want to hear the reality. He fell back on the funny stories of camp life that never failed to satisfy. He evaded any questions about his plans and glanced around the room for the one man he needed to speak with first, his father.

It was some time before he could escape. Rosemarie looked up with a glance that warmed his heart, before turning to grin at something his grandmother said. He would give a lot to know what the women were up to, especially after his grandfather, who was leaning over them, winked at him.

Harry went to the kitchen that haunted his dreams during the worst of the war and inhaled deeply; the scent of his grandmother's Christmas cakes and cinnamon buns were a balm to his soul.

And he found his father, watching the boys play cards. *At last!*

The old man raised his head and smiled, indicating with a nod that Harry should follow him into the mudroom off the back porch.

When did his hair go so gray?

Harry followed him out and moved aside so his father could shut the door for a bit of privacy. Things were better between them, but they had been stiff with each other when Harry and Rosemarie first arrived. Harry worried how he would take his latest news.

Father put a finger to his lips and reached down in a Wellington boot next to the door to pull out a flask of whisky, a favorite hiding place in the house of Harry's abstemious Methodist grandmother.

"She knows where you hide it," Harry said, taking the tumbler his father handed him. "She always did."

"Don't be a spoilsport, Harry. Tell me about Ottawa."

Right to the point. That's Father.

"There isn't much to tell. We have an apartment. I'm enrolled for next semester."

His father beamed at him. "What are you taking?"

They had come to the point. "English," Harry said.

"Latin?"

"French." Harry took a deep swallow of the whisky and put it down. "And educational theory. I'm going to be a teacher." He held his father's eyes, waiting for an argument.

"Can you support your family on a teacher's salary?" His father studied him, but Harry didn't see the argumentation in his eyes he once did.

Or perhaps I'm the one who has changed.

"Well enough. What I want is to write." He cleared his throat and said more emphatically, "I'm going to write."

William Wheatly looked surprised by Harry's revelation. "I thought you wanted to be a farmer."

Harry laughed ruefully. "So did I, but I considered what you said about the backbreaking part. I've always wanted to write." He picked up the glass and sipped it this time. "The thing is Father, the war is still in me. I have to get it out."

His father swallowed hard, sympathy naked in his eyes. "There are stories the world needs to hear, Harry," he said. "Perhaps you're the one to tell them."

The two men held one another's gaze for a long moment in perfect accord, interrupted only when the door burst open.

"Harry, my cousins—they said we are cousins now, aren't we —they taught me how to play euchre, and I almost won," Marcel exclaimed. "Come and watch." He grabbed Harry's hand and pulled him to the door.

As he stepped past, Harry's father gripped his shoulder briefly, then let him go.

THE END

AUTHOR'S NOTE

American readers will be familiar with *Taps* with its distinctive three-note opening—the traditional end-of-day bugle call associated with the funerals of the fallen. *The Last Post*, with its similar role, will be more familiar to British and Commonwealth readers. Its first two notes (the second mournful one held for a long space) are distinctive and quickly recognized by those who know it. It is the bugle call Harry heard crossing the Somme.

As always, I have attempted to be as historically accurate as possible in this story. The capture of Vimy Ridge, at the end of the day, had little strategic importance in the war as a whole, because the larger British and French operation failed. For Canadians, whose determination and valor had been put to the test and come out victorious, it had enormous symbolic importance. They came out from under the shadow of Britain. As Brigadier-General A.E. Ross declared after the war, "in those few minutes I witnessed the birth of a nation."

I based private Willard's actions that day on those of Jeremiah Jones, a black soldier from Nova Scotia. Like Willard, Jones was recommended for a Distinguished Conduct Medal but did not receive it in his lifetime. He finally received recognition for his actions in 2010.

Women engaged in all sorts of war work in France, Germany, Britain, and America. Uniform workshops existed, but the one in Amiens is purely a product of my imagination.

The Royal Engineers (Postal Section) was a unit subsumed into the British Army, but actually under the management of the British General Post Office. It had a massive mail sorting operation in London and Army Post offices (APO) in Le Havre, Boulogne, and Calais and a fleet of trucks for distribution. It appears to have been remarkably efficient, handling up to twelve million overseas letters a week sometimes. I think I can be excused for suggesting that mail inside civilian France may have been a bit more problematic.

The unrest and unruliness of the Canadian troops at Kinmel actually happened. There was, in fact, a riot in March 1919 over repatriation delays. It happened while Harry was in France. Over 54,000 war brides and dependents were repatriated to Canada in 1919. There was undoubtedly a formal procedure for their repatriation, but I was unable to locate details and had to make them up based on typical military rules and processes.

I hope the conclusion of Harry and Rosemarie's journey satisfies my readers.

ABOUT THE AUTHOR

Caroline Warfield grew up in a peripatetic army family and had a varied career (largely centered on libraries and technology) before retiring to the urban wilds of Eastern Pennsylvania. She is ever a traveler and adventurer, enamored of owls, books, history, and beautiful gardens (but not the act of gardening). She is married to a prince among men.

For more about Caroline
Website: http://www.carolinewarfield.com/

facebook.com/carolinewarfield7

twitter.com/CaroWarfield

instagram.com/carowarfield

bookbub.com/authors/caroline-warfield

OTHER BOOKS BY CAROLINE WARFIELD

The Dangerous Series (1816-1821)

Dangerous Works

A little Greek is one thing; the art of love is another. Only Andrew ever tried to teach Georgiana both.

Dangerous Weakness

A marquess who never loses control and a very independent woman spark conflict until revolution, politics, and pirates force them to work together.

Dangerous Secrets

When Jamie fled to Rome to hide his shame, he didn't expect a vicar's daughter and imp of a niece to take over his life. Will his secrets destroy their chance at love?

The Children of Empire Series (1832-1840)

The Renegade Wife

A desperate woman on the run with her children finds shelter with a reclusive businessman in the Canadian wilderness. His heart isn't as hard as he thought, and when she disappears again, he'll do anything to protect her.

The Reluctant Wife

A disgraced Bengal army officer finds himself responsible for two unexpected daughters and a headstrong, interfering,—but attractive— widow. This time, failure is not an option.

The Unexpected Wife

The Duke of Murnane seeks escape in service to the crown in the drug-ridden, contentious port of Canton, only to find his problems waiting at the end of the earth. Can love bring him back?

The Holiday Collection

Lady Charlotte's Christmas Vigil

Love is the best medicine, and the sweetest things in life are worth the wait, especially at Christmastime in Venice for a stranded English Lady and a handsome physician.

An Open Heart

She may not celebrate the same holiday as others at the Regency house party, but the banker's daughter knows she can treasure her heritage and still reach out to people of different traditions. If only she can convince her beloved to have an open heart!

A Dangerous Nativity

With Christmas coming, can the Earl of Chadbourn repair his widowed sister's damaged estate, and far more damaged family? Dare he hope for love in the bargain?

(Prequel to both the Dangerous and Children of Empire series)

Anthologies including Caroline's novellas

A Holiday in Bath

Holly and Hopeful Hearts

Never Too Late

Follow Your Star Home

Valentines From Bath

For more information see Carolines bookshelf:

https://www.carolinewarfield.com/bookshelf/